TWO MEN:

He was . . .

Kingsley Cusack, Jr. Born 1965, Cincinnati, Ohio, United States of the Americas. Father, Kingsley Cusack; Mother, Dorothy Ellen Dodge. Education: Bachelor's Degree in Anthropology, University City of Cincinnati; Master's degree and Doctor's degree in Ethnology, University City of Princeton. Author of: *The Montezuma Myth* and *The Way of the Mayan*. Residence, Apartment 1324, The Longfellow Building, University City of Princeton.

He was . . .

Phipe Horatius Cocles. Born in the year of Rome 216 (553 B.C.), in Rome. Father, Celer Horatius Cocles, of the Horatian gens of the Ramnes tribe of Rome. Mother, Larthia Camna of the Camna gens of the Etruscan city of Caere, niece of the Lucumo. Education: private tutor in Rome and the Etruscan schools of Caere. Military training: the Cohort of Marcus Valerius. Residence, the Palatine Hill, Rome. Honors: the title Hero of the Sublican Bridge. A brazen statue raised in the Forum.

THE COMPUTER MADE THEM ONE.

PERCHANCE TO DREAM

by
Mack Reynolds

ace books
A Division of Charter Communications Inc.
A GROSSET & DUNLAP COMPANY
1120 Avenue of the Americas
New York, New York 10036

PERCHANCE TO DREAM

Copyright © 1977 by Mack Reynolds

An ACE Book

First Ace Printing: December 1977

Cover art by Dean Ellis

Published simultaneously in Canada

Printed in U.S.A.

Lars Porsenna of Clusium
        By the nine gods he swore
That the great house of Tarquin
        Should suffer wrong no more.

Shame on the false Etruscan
        Who lingers in his home,
When Porsenna of Clusium
        Is on the march for Rome.

To eastward and to westward
        Have spread the Tuscan bands;
Nor house, nor fence, nor dovecot
        In Crustumerium stands.
Verbenna down to Ostia
        Hath wasted all the plain;
Astur has stormed Janiculum,
        And the stout guards are slain.

Up spoke the consul roundly,
        "The bridge must strait go down;
For if they once may win the bridge,
        What hope to save the town?"

Then out spake brave Horatius,
        The Captain of the Gate:
"To every man upon this earth
        Death cometh soon or late.

"Hew down the bridge, Sir Consul,
        With all the speed ye may;
I with two more to help me,
        Will hold the foe in play.
In yon strait path a thousand
        May well be stopped by three.
Now who will stand on either hand,
        And keep the bridge with me?"

Meanwhile the Tuscan army,
    Right glorious to behold,
Came flashing back the noonday light,
Rank behind rank, like surges bright
    On a broad sea of gold.

And forth three chiefs came spurring
    Before that deep array;
To earth they sprang, their swords they drew,
And lifted high their shields, and flew
    To win the narrow way.

Then Ocnus of Falerii
    Rushed on the Roman three,
And Lausulus of Urgo,
    The rover of the sea;
And Aruns of Volsinium
    Who slew the great wild boar. . .

But hark! the cry is Astur:
    And lo! the ranks divide;
And the great Lord of Luna
    Comes with his stately stride.
Quoth he, "The she wolf's litter
    Stands savagely at bay:
But will ye dare to follow,
    If Astur clears the way?"

"And see," cried brave Horatius, "the welcome,
    Fair guests, that waits you here!
What noble Lucumo comes next
    To taste our Roman cheer?"

Was none who would be foremost
    To lead such dire attack:
But those behind cried, "Forward!"
    And those before cried, "Back!"

"Come back, come back, Horatius!"
    Loud cried the Fathers all.

"Back Lartius! back, Herminius!
    Back ere the ruin fall!"

Back darted Spurius Lartius;
    Herminius darted back:
And as they passed, beneath their feet
    They felt the timbers crack.
But when they turned their faces,
    And on the further shore
Saw brave Horatius stand alone,
    They would have crossed once more.

Alone stood brave Horatius,
    But constant still in mind;
Thrice thirty thousand foes before,
    And the broad flood behind.

"Oh, Tiber! father Tiber!
    To whom the Romans pray,
A Roman's life, A Roman's arms,
    Take thou in charge this day!"

So he spake and speaking sheathed
    the god sword by his side,
And with his harness on his back,
    Plunged headlong in the tide.

And when above the surges
    They saw his crest appear,
All Rome sent forth a rapturous cry,
And even the ranks of Tuscany
    Could scarce forbear to cheer.

"Heaven help him!" quoth Lars Porsenna,
    "And bring him safe to shore;
For such a gallant feat of arms
    Was never seen before."

                The Lays of Ancient Rome

                by Lord Macaulay

Chapter One

Yucatan/Princeton—Kingsley Cusack

Dr. Kingsley Cusack was somewhere in the vicinity of forty, though he didn't look it. He had an open, boyish face, thick blondish hair, and a wiry figure that showed no signs of middle-age spread. Now he was taking a farewell look at the so-called House of the Nuns, in Uxmal, Yucatan. Cusack had spent a good deal of time with the building and he hoped that the paper he had written on it would cause a stir in academic circles, particularly among archeologists and anthropologists, possibly even to the point of his winning his academician's degree, which might give him a chance at a teaching job.

His contention was that the building had nothing whatsoever to do with the Mayan version of nuns—if there had ever been such a thing. It was his claim that the Mayans and that the seventy-six apartments had once housed a gens and had no connection with religion. Such community houses, or their ruins, were to be found stretched from Taos, New Mexico, and Zuni, Arizona, all the way through Mexico proper and down into Central America.

It wasn't going to be a popular view, this suggesting that the Mayans practiced primitive communism in their manner of living, but he was stuck with it, because he believed it.

He turned and retraced his way to his electrosteamer hover-car, piled in, activated it, and dropped the lift lever. Driving manually, since the roads weren't automated in Yucatan, he put his foot on the accelerator and started off for Merida, fifty-eight miles to the north.

Kingsley Cusack was both glad and sad to be leaving Yucatan. Eight years in one vicinity was enough, no matter how devoted you were to your project. He suspected that currently he knew as much about the Mayans as anyone living, and his book, *The Way of the Mayans*, with any luck at all, should become the definitive work on that people. But he didn't mind getting back to civilization and to the desirable aspects of the scholarly life in a university city.

He already had his bags and things in the car. The bulky collection of books and other papers he had shipped. He dropped the car off at the car pool from which he had rented it and took public transportation to the shuttleport near Progresso. He took the shuttle rocket to the shuttleport in what had once been northern New Jersey, and then public transportation in the underground to the Princeton University City, where he had made his permanent home since he had gone there seeking his master's as a young man.

At the university's transportation center, he disembarked and took one of the metros to the Longfellow Building. He got out on the basement level which housed the car pool as well as public transportation facilities and took an elevator to the 132nd floor of the high-rise.

The Longfellow Building, one of the dozen high-rises of the university city, was a two-tower affair and in all could accommodate as many as twenty thousand persons in its some five thousand apartments. It could, but it seldom did. Many of the suites were occupied by no more than a single person, as was Kingsley Cusack's. The building was a small city in itself, containing entertainment facilities, restaurants, a large supermarket-cum-department-store, and even a well-staffed hospital. The size of the total staff can be imagined when it is considered that there were a hundred security employees alone.

Kingsley Cusack's automated apartment was moderate sized since he was a solo. Not that he minded. His field trips were so lengthy that he had lived here comparatively little since he had taken his doctorate. In the past eight years he doubted if he had spent more than two or three months in the university city. But it was gratifying to have a place for your books, your art objects, the artifacts you had gathered on your expeditions.

He entered his home now feeling very pleased to be back. If he never saw another mosquito in his life, and never had another case of heat rash, and never got scared by another snake, it was all right with him. And he was tired of Mayan food. The archeology authorities who dominated the area made a fetish of keeping it primitive and uncontaminated. He was all set for some gourmet meals from the automated kitchens of the Longfellow Building, down in the bowels of the high-rise.

In fact, he decided to have a quick drink before unpacking, and then to dial for lunch. But that wasn't to be. The phone screen on his desk buzzed and he went to answer it, rather surprised to get a call this soon after his arrival.

The screen lit up and the beaming face of Academician Bryce Norman was there. He was about five years older than Kingsley and for a long time had been his best friend as well as his mentor. The years hadn't dealt with him quite so kindly as with Kingsley, in view of his sedentary life, and he was a bit heavy of jowls, a bit rounded of paunch, though his eyes were shone bright and pierced deep.

He said, "King! I heard on the news that you were scheduled to return today. Come on up!"

As a matter of fact, Kingsley Cusack would just as well have taken a rain check, but Norman was important to him beyond the friendship. He was the head of the archeology department and threw a lot of weight.

"Be right up," Kingsley said. "Have a drink ready for me, and don't dare make it tequila or mescal."

He flicked off the phone and headed for the door. He hoped Norman was having him for lunch. He hadn't eaten since that morning when he'd been in Yucatan.

Academician Bryce Norman lived in one of the more rarified apartments of the building. Rank had its privileges even in a University City, and the higher your rank, the higher your apartment. Kingsley had always claimed that on a clear day you could see New York from Bryce Norman's digs.

He took the elevator and was met by the academician at his door, two pleasantly chilled highball glasses in hand.

Bryce Norman smiled and handed one of them over. "No tequila," he said. "Stone Age Scotch imported directly from the land of peat and heather, bagpipes and lassies."

Kingsley tried to look soulful and followed the other back to his escape sanctum, where it was impossible to be bothered.

When they were seated, Academician Norman said, "Damn, but it's been a long time, King. How long were you on that Yucatan expedition? I haven't seen you more than briefly for years."

"Almost eight years. It's a bag of mine that I expect to retain. I like to saturate myself in one period, devoting my time to nothing else and remaining on the scene. When I finally finish my research and my book, I completely drop the period and never dip into it again. Then I take up another period."

The academician said, "I read your *The Way of the Mayan*. It's already in the data banks." He held up his glass. "Cheers, cheers."

"Cheers," Kingsley said, taking back a slug of the Scotch and water. The other had been right. It was Stone Age and undoubtedly the pure stuff, rather than the usual blend the Scots exported. He said cautiously, "What did you think of it, Bryce?"

The other considered, before saying, "I think it's a bit on the controversial side."

Kingsley Cusack was unhappy. "You don't think there's any chance of my taking my· academician's degree on the strength of it? Good God, eight years of concentrated research. No wonder it's controversial: Most of the former material is tripe."

Norman said unhappily, "Your *Montezuma Myth* was along the same line, King. Controversial. Perhaps that's why the powers-that-be, here at the university, give you the silent treatment. Older men, in positions of authority and wishing to retain them, are inclined to be conservative. There are far too few teaching jobs to go around. I've been bucking for you, of course, but others are involved." Then he said, after taking a pull at the drink. "So your eight years with the Mayans are up and you put them completely behind you. What's your next period to be, King?"

Kingsley was unhappy still about what his friend had said about his first two books, but he answered, "I think I'll go on over to Rome and its area and spend the next six or eight years working on the period when the Etruscan reges were expelled from Rome and the Republic was instituted."

His friend sipped at his whisky again. He hesitated for a moment, then said, "There's no need to go to Italy."

Kingsley shook his head. "That's the way I work," he told the other. "On the scene. When I did my book on the Aztecs, I stayed in Mexico City and its vicinity. With the Mayans, of course, I stayed in Yucatan, though I made a few side trips to Guatamala."

"Ummm," the academician nodded. "But there have been some changes."

6

"What changes?" Kingsley said, frowning.

The academician smiled at him, somewhat slyly. "You were gone eight years, eh, and stayed in a remote area? King, haven't you heard about the knowledge explosion? That human knowledge is doubling every eight or ten years?"

Kingsley scoffed and drank more of the excellent Scotch. He said, "Yes, and no doubt it applies to such sciences as physics, chemistry, biology. But it's another thing when you get to such slow-paced fields as archeology and anthropology. You don't get spectacular breakthroughs in our sciences."

His host was still smiling, his former hesitation evidently forgotten. He said, "What would you say the last really big breakthrough in archeology was?"

Kingsley Cusack thought about it. He snorted before saying, "In actuality, the last really big breakthrough was probably carbon dating, and that happened long before I was even born. You just don't have breakthroughs in the social sciences."

His friend laughed softly and pointed. "Meet the most recent major breakthrough in the fields of anthropology, history, and archeology, King." He was pointing at something which looked remarkably like a sterile, cold metalic coffin, with the lid off.

Kingsley had noted the thing when he had first entered the room but had refrained from saying anything about it. The oblong box, which lay on a heavy table, was about seven feet in length. Now that he took a closer look at it, he could make out some dials and switches built into its side, and next to it was what looked like a microphone.

"What in the world are you talking about?" he asked.

"The dream programmer."

Kingsley Cusack looked at his friend, waiting for him to go on. The academician got up and took Kingsley's nearly empty glass from his hand and went over to the autobar to dial fresh drinks.

"It's something the computer technicians and the biologists hit up on a short time ago. It's been kept hush-hush. And for good reason. There is only the one in the whole University City."

"Dream programmer? That doesn't make too much sense. You mean it can give you canned dreams?"

The other frowned slightly. He said, "Well, in a way, but not exactly. The term 'dream' is actually a misnomer. We should call the device something else. Actually, what it does is imprint something on your mind, an experience that you've never had. But once imprinted, it becomes part of your memory, as valid a memory as any others you might have."

Kingsley was still at sea. He said, "That sounds fascinating and undoubtedly opens up a whole new frontier for entertainment. I would think it would play havoc with such entertainment fields as tri-di, or even novels. But what in the world has it got to do with history, archeology, and anthropology?"

The academician smiled again and said, "You have, of course, read the account of the Crucifixion and Resurrection?"

"There are three accounts in the Synoptic Gospels and they all differ."

The academician nodded. "Indeed they do. How

would you like to, ah, 'dream' that you were the disciple Peter and witness the whole thing?''

Kingsley scowled at the other again and said, ''What would that have to do with the study of history?''

The academician nodded before saying, ''The dream programmer is hooked into the International Data Banks, which by now, of course, contain every bit of knowledge available. Every bit. Your supposed dream contains everything that is known about the Crucifixion. Not only the material in the three Gospels, but every scrap of information, from every part of the world, that would add to the authenticity of your dream. As a scholar, you realize that there are Apocrypha existing on the early Christians ranging from a few lines in some remote town such as Timbuktu, to whole books of the Bible in such lands as Ethiopia with its Coptic Christianity. All this the computers consult before working such material as is most valid into your programmed dream.''

Kingsley had taken the new drink from his host and took a sip from it while the other was reseating himself. He said, ''I still don't get it. Receiving such a dream wouldn't add anything to currently known data. All the material that could possibly be included in the dream is already in the data banks and a scholar can seek it out. The mystery of what really happened to Jesus would still be a mystery.''

His friend beamed at him, characteristically, and asked, ''King, what do you know about intuition?''

''Intuition? You mean direct perception of truths, facts, and so forth, independently of any reasoning process . . . pure, untaught, noninferential knowl-

9

edge? I don't know anything about it, except that it evidently exists. Does anybody know anything about it?''

The academician put his glass down and placed his fingertips together. "It works something like this," he said. "Suppose you have a problem, the answer to which contains ten elements. You have only some of these elements at your disposal. You examine the first, second, third, fourth and fifth. Possibly, as you are examining the sixth, intuition comes to you. You have the answer. Why? We're not sure, but one explanation is that buried in your subconscious was more information on the subject than you knew you had. Your brain is a computer and its data banks contain a great deal of material, some of which you are not aware you possess. When some of this is utilized, bingo, we call it intuition."

"All right," Kingsley said. "But what has all this got to do with programmed dreams?"

Norman nodded. "We now get to the nitty-gritty. While you were in Yucatan, some computer chaps came up with a new model which is quite astounding. They call it an Intuition Computer. It is, of course, hooked into the International Data Banks. Take that example I just used of the ten-element problem. A human brain might come up with the ultimate answer after contemplating five or six of the elements. The Intuitive Computer needs as few as three."

"Holy smokes."

"Yes. Holy smokes. So this is what happens. In your dream of the Crucifixion, the Intuitive Computer is at work. We have only a few valid elements of the

Crucifixion story, but they are probably enough for the programmed dream to give you the accurate story. And, in your dream, you witness it.''

"Holy smokes," Kingsley said again.

"Yes, indeed," the academician said. He looked over at the dream machine and said thoughtfully, "It is probably the most dangerous invention ever made by man."

His younger guest stared at him. "Dangerous? Why it's wonderful!"

"It's more dangerous to the human race than the worst narcotics ever developed. Worse that the opiates, even the more refined ones such as morphine and heroin."

Chapter Two

Princeton—Kingsley Cusack

Kingsley was still staring. He said, "I . . . I simply don't understand."

The other nodded, as though not at all surprised. "You haven't thought it through, as yet. But earlier you mentioned the entertainment value. And that's the crux. For instance, the Mongolian conqueror, Tamerlane, had a harem of more than two hundred women. They were the most beautiful women to be found anywhere in the world, ranging from England to China. He made it a top priority project, securing these beauties. With the dream programmer, you could dream that you were Tamerlane and spend an evening in his harem."

Kingsley Cusack hadn't slept with a woman for months. He had to laugh. "Good grief, you eunuch, what would be wrong with that?"

His friend looked at him oddly. He said, "Or you could dream you were the Pharoah husband of Queen Nefertiti, who some claim to have been the most beautiful woman ever to live, and her bust in the Berlin

Museum bears that out. Or you could be Mark Antony and barge down the Nile with Cleopatra.''

Kingsley Cusack blinked at him; some of the implications were beginning to come through.

The Academician went on. ''If this dream programmer was released to the public, how many men would you say would be satisfied with sleeping with their wives, or mistresses?'' Or how many women would be satisfied to sleep with their present-day lovers when Achilles or even Apollo were available?''

''Hold on, now,'' Kingsley protested. ''Those two were mythological.''

''That doesn't make any difference. The computers put together all the material pertaining even to a fictional scene and character, and program you a dream that you have outlined for them. And, remember, when you awaken, you think it truly happened.''

Kingsley whistled softly between his teeth. ''What else?''

''Take those drugs I mentioned. With the dream programmer you could dream of being hung up on heroin. You would have all the pleasures and sensations of taking the evil narcotic, but when you awakened there would be no aftereffects, as far as physiology is concerned, nor could you become addicted. You could experiment with every drug in the book, from the legendary soma to the sacred mushrooms of Mexico. And you would never become addicted. For that matter, you could go on a tremendous drunk, perhaps attending a Roman Saturnalia, or a Viking Wassail, and when you awakened you would have no hangover or any other physical results, save your memory of what transpired. Or, suppose you are a gourmet. You could dream yourself Nero and attend one of his fabulous banquets, hummingbird tongues and all that sort of thing.''

''Holy smokes,'' Kingsley said at that one. ''Who'd want to eat in this day and age after a bit of that sort of experience?''

''Precisely,'' Bryce Norman said. ''Or take another possibility. Suppose you decided you'd like the thrill of killing your fellow man, without incurring the dim view that society usually takes of a killer. Very well, you dream you are Wild Bill Hickok, or Wyatt Earp and shoot up all of the people you wish. Obviously, you haven't really killed anyone, so no exception could be taken by legal authorities.

''To carry it still further. War has been eliminated these days. But suppose that you're fascinated by it. You have a dream programmed in which you are Julius Caesar and you fight one of his battles against Pompey. Can you imagine any contemporary experience that could even begin to rival the thrill?''

''I see what you mean.''

''Or take sports,'' the academician pressed. ''If you like mountain climbing you could be Hillary and scale Everest. If you like boxing, you can be the almost legendary Joe Louis and become world champ. Or you could be Manolete and kill bulls as they have never been killed by other matadors. You could win the Olympics in any, or all, for that matter, of the contests.''

''I'm beginning to see light,'' Kingsley murmured.

"Yes, who would bother to participate in real sports, if he could be world champion in any of them, just by taking a programmed dream? No, King, if this device is made free to the public, we will become a world of dreamers, ignoring reality."

Kingsley Cusack finished his second drink and came to his feet and paced the floor thoughtfully, his hands in his pockets. Academician Norman held his peace.

Kingsley said finally, "I begin to see why I have not even heard of the device. I wasn't much for the news, down in Yucatan, but when you first mentioned the dream programmer I was surprised that I knew nothing of it."

The other nodded. "It is one of the best-kept secrets since the Manhattan Project and its ramifications are probably just as serious."

"But you believe I could receive permission to utilize it for my research into the early Rome and the Etruscans?"

"We won't say anything about it, King," the academician told him. "It would be too complicated and you aren't even a member of the Teaching Guild. You still live on Guaranteed Annual Income, don't you?"

"Yes," Kingsley said bitterly. "And have all of my life. With the new mechanical educators, there's precious little call for teachers except on the administrative end, and that's not for me."

"All right," Norman said. "We'll work in conjunction and no one will know. I was assigned this one to experimentally research the life of the first of the great

Persian kings, Cyrus. It's slow going, since I'm trying to cover the whole span of his life. But you can be utilizing it when I'm not under.''

Kingsley didn't understand that.

The other explained. ''Eight hours is the maximum time you should be in the dream world. Time there proceeds at the same pace as it does in our own world.''

''Why only eight hours, though?''

The academician shrugged. ''Isn't it obvious? You must have time out for exercise, for your meals, for other aspects of your work, such as making notes and doing further research in the data banks. Besides, while you're under you aren't truly sleeping, you are in a sort of coma. You do not awaken refreshed; sometimes to the contrary. If a great deal was going on in your dream, you feel it psychologically. For instance, take that harem of Tamerlane's. If you spent eight hours in it, when you awakened, believe me, you would not be interested in further sex. You would feel drained, even though, in actuality, you hadn't had a true orgasm. At any rate, eight hours is all I ever take, and I suggest that you take an even shorter period for your first experiment.''

Kingsley Cusack had stopped his pacing. He said, ''Look, I'm starved and those two drinks have really whetted my appetite. Let's have a bite while I consider all that you've told me. Believe me, it all comes as a fantastic surprise.''

The academician came to his feet. ''Certainly, King. I was about to suggest it myself. Let's go into the dining room.''

Kingsley followed the older man, biting his underlip

as he went. There were so many angles to this that he didn't know where to start in examining them.

At the table, he said to the other, "You dial for me. After eight years, it's been so seldom that I've eaten anything save Yucatan food that I'd probably wind up ordering tortillas, venison *carnitas,* chilis, to be washed down with black beer."

Bryce Norman laughed. "Very well," he said. "Something different."

He didn't have to check the voluminous menu, which came in a volume as large as a telephone book of a major city. He knew exactly what he wanted and dialed it: Sauerbraten, *Kartoffelklosse*, Red Cabbage, Crisp Vegetables, and Pineapple Mousse.

He said, "We'll take you as far as we can get from Yucatan food. I've been on a bit of a Germanic binge recently. Lager beer, or wine?"

Kingsley said, "About the only decent local booze in Merida and vicinity is their dark rich beer. Wonderful. But as a change I'd like German Reisling."

"An excellent *Liebfraumilch* I know about!" Norman said enthusiastically. He dialed it.

Kingsley could see why his older friend was going to pot. He had come to love his stomach. He wondered, in inner amusement, if Bryce Norman had ever taken advantage of the dream programmer to take in one of those Roman banquet-orgies. He had a sneaking suspicion that the other had.

While they waited for the dishes and wine to be delivered from the automated kitchens in the basements of the Longfellow Building, the academician said, "I'll be using the dream programmer this afternoon. But I assume that you're somewhat tired, anyway. And also that you want to get squared away in your apartment. But what do you say that tomorrow morning you come up and we'll give you a preliminary couple of hours in it?''

"Fine. I still have my doubts about this as a valid method of research but I certainly want to try it.''

"Good. Just remember that supposedly while the device is in my hands I am pledged not to allow anyone else to utilize it. So don't mention it to anyone. Now then, who can we focus upon in the period in which you're interested? By the way, what is the exact date?''

"About 510 to 509 B.C.'' Kingsley told him. "How do you mean focus upon?''

"For historical research of this type, you should have some individual to identify with. What it amounts to is you *become* that person. For the Crucifixion story, for instance, you would become one of the disciples, or, if you wished, even Jesus himself.''

While Kingsley was thinking about that, the center of the table dropped down and returned with the Germanic lunch. The academician took up the dishes and utensils and placed them before the two of them.

Kingsley said, "Well, there was Lars Porsenna, or Lar Porsenna, who led the Etruscan armies against Rome.''

"I'm not an Etruscan specialist,'' Bryce Norman said, taking up a fork, "though I've heard the name. What do we know about him?''

Kingsley took up his knife and fork, saying, "Precious little. He was evidently the lucumo, the sort of priest-king, of either Chiusi, which the Romans called

Colusium, or Volsini. And he was evidently also the head war chief of the twelve cities of the Etruscan league.''

"Ummm. Physical description?"

"There is none, so far as I know."

''That's not so good. If you don't know any more than that you might wind up with nothing more than a fictionalized dream. You have to have a central character that the computers can go to work on. It's somewhat complicated.''

Kingsley said, frowning, "Well, there was the rex, Tarquinius Superbus, the last of the Etruscan reges of Rome. The whole war was fought because Porsenna was trying to regain his throne for him.''

"Physical description?"

''Well, no. We don't know too much more about him than we do Lars Porsenna, except that he was an old man at the time of his expulsion. His youngest son, Sextus, started the whole thing when he raped Lucretia, the daughter of a Roman patrician."

His host sighed, even as he began digging into the sauerbraten. He said, "You're going to have to have someone better than that."

Kingsley Cusack came up with an inspiration. "Horatius Cocles," he said.

Bryce Norman looked at him. "Of Horatius at the bridge fame? Did that really happen?"

''Evidently,'' Kingsley told him. "Plutarch, Livy, and Polybius all record the story, although the accounts differ.''

"Do any of them give a physical description of him?"

"It seems to me that at least Plutarch does. In his chapter on Poplicola."

Next to the table was a stand with a phone screen. Bryce Norman turned half around and dialed it. "Plutarch, eh?" he said. "We'll see what they've got in the library data banks."

The book flashed on the screen and he touched a stud to open it to the table of contents, then flicked the pages until he reached the chapter on Poplicola.

He read aloud: ". . . the Romans, being dismayed, retreated into the city for their security, and Rome was in great hazard of being taken, the enemy forcing their way onto the wooden bridge, where Horatius Cocles, seconded by two of the first men in Rome, Herminius and Lartius, made head against them. Horatius obtained this name from the loss of one of his eyes in the war, or, as others write, from the depressure of his nose, which, leaving nothing in the middle to separate them, made both eyes appear as one; and hence, intending to say Cyclops, by mispronounciation they called him Cocles. This Cocles kept the bridge, and held back the enemy, till his own party broke it down behind him, and then with his armor dropped into the river and swam to the hither side, with a wound in his hip from a Tuscan spear. Poplicola, admiring his courage, proposed at once that the Romans should every one make him a present of a day's provisions, and afterwards gave him as much land as he could plow around in one day, and besides erected a brazen statue to his honor in the Temple of Vulcan, as a requital for the lameness caused by his wound."

The academician finished and said, "Not too very

20

much but we'll check the others as well, later. Tomorrow morning when you come, have all the information on this Horatius that you can find."

Kingsley Cusack shook his head. "I still don't see how the computers can come up with material that I couldn't find on my own in their data banks."

"Put it this way," the other said. "It's known that the Etruscan women wore silk as early as the sixth century B.C. It was available at that time only from China or Japan. Is it not to be assumed that there is currently in the International Data Banks, buried away in the archives from early Chinese sources, information, no matter how little, on the Etruscans? And from those people in between that must have dealt with the trade? How do we know what remote archives in Turkestan might have scraps of such information? When the Intuitive Computer goes to work on your dream, it will seek out every such scrap of information and utilize that which is most suitable."

Kingsley shrugged. "As I say, I'll most gladly give it a try."

They both went back to their food.

In the morning, Kingsley repaired again to the apartment of his friend and mentor. He had spent several hours accumulating all the information that was known of the historic Horatius Cocles and had been able to locate several other small items to add to the Livy, Plutarch, and Polybius accounts. He had gotten onto his vocotyper and done it all up in notes, as instructed by the academician.

The other led him into the escape room and to the dream programmer. Bryce Norman said, "If you intend your researches to extend over a period of time, then I suggest you keep your dreaming in chronological order, otherwise it can get confusing.''

"All right," Kingsley said nervously. "I'll take this first two hours in the youth of Horatius. That will put it back into the times when the Tarquins were still in power. Listen, can anything go wrong?"

Academician Norman laughed at him. "Not really," he said. "The only case I ever heard of was an associate who decided to study Billy the Kid, that pimply faced juvenile delinquent who never killed a man in a fair fight in his life. At any rate, the dream was a success and he relived the siege of the Maxwell house quite successfully. He decided to continue to investigate William Bonney's life and dream of his escape from prison, during which he killed two defenseless men. But instead of that period in Billy's life, this chap again dreamed of the siege he had already relived. And from then on, nothing availed him. Every time he tried to get a programmed dream, he redreamed that event. What was worse, the dream began to come to him every night in his real dreams." He laughed again. "What a fate."

"What's so funny?" Kingsley growled. "That's all I'd have to have is something like that happen to me. Let's get this show on the road before I back down."

The other instructed him. He had to read all the material he had on Horatius into the machine's speaker. He then had to request a two hour dream based on the youth of Horatius. He then had to stretch out in the coffin-like metallic box and allow Norman to lay electrodes on his closed eyes and to the nape of his neck, then to both his wrists and his ankles.

"You can do this yourself the next time," the old man told him. "These give you low-frequency pulses applied to the cerebral cortex and portions of the spine. And now I'll give you this hypodermic shot."

"Oh, great," Kingsley muttered. "Rome, here I come."

But it was not in Rome that he came alive.

Chapter Three

Caere—Phipe Horatius Cocles

Suddenly, I seemed to have a dual mind. Another mind prying in mine. It was not particularly alarming. It seemed not only to be aware of what I was about, but also to dig into my memories.

Thus it found that I am Phipe Horatius Cocles, son of Celer Horatius Cocles, of the Horatian gens of the Romnes tribe of Rome, and once Roman ambassador to Caere, and of Larthia Camna of the Camna gens of that Etruscan city, who is now passed away.

On my fourteenth year I was sent to the city of my mother's birth to receive higher education, since it was famed for its university.

As a Camna born, I was considered a member of that gens since descent among the Etruscans is in the female line, though in Rome it is in the male. Thus, while my father's family was not patrician, my mother's was that which invariably provided the lucumo of Caere and I couldn't have had more family prestige.

Hence, as a student, I could have lived in the former home of my mother, but it would have been too far from the school buildings. Some of the boys lived in simple dormitories, but, since I was a Camna, I was quartered with only one other lad, Astur of Volterra, who was my equal in rank.

Although he was only fifteen, he was the largest boy in the school, well over six feet, and must have carried at least two hundred pounds. Astur was a giant born, and, as often among men who are so big that there can be no question of their strength, he was inordinarily mellow of nature and had no tendency toward belligerence. It was thought that one day Astur might be elected by the Volterrans to take his uncle's place as lucumo and thus he was in Caere to be educated. He was by no means alone in this position. Octavius Mamilius of Tusculum, who was from one of the Latin cities to the south of Rome, had the quarters immediately next to ours. A member of the Mamilian gens and about the same age as we, it was expected that he, too, might one day be elected rex of his city. He shared his quarters with Sextus Tarquin, son of the rex of Rome.

We four soon made a close-knit group, although Sextus was never quite so much a member of our clique as were we other three. In fact, Aruns of Volsini, who was quartered with three other boys, was closer to us than Sextus, a somewhat sulky lad who spent much time in his own company. Aruns was of that city Volsini, in which the Etruscan Confederation was centered, that is, where the grove of the god Voltumna is located near Lake Bolsena. He, himself, was a boy who had difficulty concentrating on his studies; his heart was up in the hills, running the deer, or out on the sea in a small boat, angling for fish.

We were still young enough, though almost fully grown physically, to occasionally play at Greek and Trojan in mock warfare, nor were we discouraged by our instructors, one of whom, a dour veteran of many a battle, growled that in his opinion we boys often conducted a play campaign, or evolved tactics or strategy in game, superior to those he had often followed in the field under supposedly competent officers.

At any rate, at the time my strange dual mind came about we were about to fight a mock battle supposedly between the Etruscans and the Celts.

We students had enlisted the support of possibly as many as a hundred Caere boys of our own age, all equipped with the wooden practice swords and shields such as we used in the gymnasium and such as the other lads used in drill under Etruscan veterans preparing them for manhood and military duties. When sides were evenly divided, we both had an imposing array of soldiers and I, remembering similar escapades in Rome, had about decided that we'd be lucky if the whole matter ended with no more than two or three broken limbs. Boys of fourteen, though barely out of childhood, can often boast physiques not far inferior to those of their fathers. However, it did not turn out as disastrously as I had expected.

I was to be found, a subchief in command of ten, in the ranks of the Celts, a people of whom I knew next to nothing. Aruns was our war chief and most of our school clique supported him. The other side, the Etruscans, was led by a town boy named Gargo who had been chosen by his fellows due to qualities of leadership and personal elan. Both sides formed into ranks, surprisingly military-like considering our years, and grimly headed for each other. On the face of it, mutual massacre was inevitable.

But at this point the enemy's lines opened and one of their number stepped forward a few steps and shouted, "I am Ruga of Arpinum of the Alvethna gens and hence of lucumo lineage and challenge to personal combat a chief of equal rank!"

Whereupon his comrades behind him beat their swords upon their shields in a deafening approval, and, after a moment, the boys of our own brigade began to do the same. Sextus stood beside me and I looked at him questioningly, but he shrugged his shoulders, obviously as mystified as I. At this time neither of us had been in Caere for very long.

Aruns, however, was well acquainted with the procedure and called a council of his subchiefs. There was a short discussion and then Mamilius was sent forth after being quickly briefed by Aruns on the niceties of the matter.

He advanced until within a few yards of Ruga of Arpinum, stopped and held his sword in salute and called, "I am Octavius Mamilius of Tusculum, of the Mamilian gens and son of the rex!" Which rank was evidently notable enough for his challenger who promptly set upon Mamilius with fine ardor. Alas for his heroic pretensions, he lasted not a moment with our champion swordsman. Manilius took his opponent's first hefty swing on the shield, twisted his body in such fashion that the other lad stumbled by, and then banged brave Ruga on the crown and evidently so painfully that the boy dropped sword and shield and held his head with both hands in agony. Mamilius picked up his opponent's weapon, as loot of war, and, grinning widely, returned to our ranks.

It was all received with such approval, especially by our side, obviously, that nothing would do but that Sextus must step forth and bawl his own challenge to the enemy ranks.

"I am Sextus Tarquin of the Tarquin gens, son of the rex of Rome and direct descendant of Tarchon, founder of all Etruria, and challenge to personal combat a chief of equal rank!"

Looking at it truthfully, I suspect that Sextus, never particularly aggressive in the rougher sports, had succumbed to the opportunity to call attention to himself by his impressive lineage. Be that as may, he didn't have to back up his challenge, for, to his surprise, as well as mine, the chiefs of the enemy gathered to debate the matter and finally sent forth an unarmed lad as a fetial, a woolen fillet over his head in approved fashion of the mature ambassadors.

The fetial called to Aruns, and to Sextus, with a considerable dignity, eyes and face grave, "We have held council among us and find no chieftain of sufficient rank to meet the challenge, and so retire from the field in defeat." Whereupon he returned to his comrades and their army marched off in good order.

Aruns scowled at Sextus. "You've ended the whole thing. You shouldn't have added that about Tarchon. How could any good Etruscan claim equal rank?"

But Sextus was as taken aback by the development as I was. "What could I have said?" he complained.

Our army, set for fray but a moment ago, was breaking up into groups, most of the lads undoubtedly secretly happy that it was over without the bruises and cuts to which they had reconciled themselves. Their side had triumphed with little effort but considerable glory. Many of them gathered around Mamilius to thump him on the back, but they avoided Sextus, evidently disapproving of his boastfulness.

Mamilius and Astur came over to where I stood with Sextus, and the two Etruscans grinned at us. "That's the way they did it in the old days," Aruns was explaining. "I think it comes down from even before the time of Troy."

He looked at Sextus and answered the question the other had asked earlier. "If you'd just challenged as son of the rex of Rome, they'd have sent out an opponent who was the nephew of some lucumo."

"I didn't even know," Sextus said sullenly.

I looked at Astur. "Why didn't you challenge?"

The giant youth grinned, uncomfortably. "I couldn't. There wasn't anybody my size in their ranks. They would have sent out some little fellow who would have had to take a beating."

Chapter Four

Princeton—Kingsley Cusack

Suddenly, it was over. Kingsley Cusack brought up his hands and moved away the electrodes over his eyes. He was breathing deeply.

Academician Norman had been seated at his desk, concentrating on the screen of his library booster. Now he looked up, saw that Kingsley was back in the present, and stood to go over and help him with the other wiring, so that he could get out of the coffin-like box.

"Holy smokes," Kingsley said, "give me a drink. Anything."

"What? At this time of the day?" his friend said mockingly.

"I don't care what the hell time of day it is," Kingsley Cusack muttered. The younger man strode over to the escape room's autobar and dialed himself a double brandy. When it came, he took it up and knocked it back in one jolt.

He turned to the other. "Look, how much of that really happened?"

"None of it," the academician said flatly.

"Listen," Kingsley said, still breathing deeply. "That memory is as clear to me as any experience I have ever had in my life."

Bryce Norman settled back into his swivel chair again. He put this fingertips together. "I know," he said. "The first time I dreamt, I was Lee at Gettysburg. In my true life, of course, I have never seen any combat whatsoever, never fired a gun; in fact, I have never seen a gun outside a museum. But in my dream I was Lee, giving orders to Longstreet and Hill, directing Pickett to make his famous final charge, which eventually broke the back of the Confederacy. Yes, I suspect my reaction was even stronger than your own. I had two horses shot from under me."

Kingsley protested, "But I was in an Etruscan city. It was real. It couldn't have been a fake, couldn't have been a mockup, or something. The boys I talked to, the clothes we wore, all were *real.*"

Bryce Norman shook his head. "Only in your mind. The computers drew upon every scrap of information they have on the Etruscan civilization. Where they lacked, they drew upon the Intuitive Computer to fill out their information."

"But how could they know such details as that when Etruscan boys played at war they issued personal challenges to each other, based on the family rank?"

The academician shrugged. "I wouldn't know."

Kingsley Cusack paced the floor in irritation. "But I tell you, it was as though I was in that boy's skull. I had all of his memories. I knew everything he knew. Even things that had happened before he was born but that he

31

had been told about. For instance, his father was Roman ambassador, or military attaché, to Caere at the time of the Carthaginian and Etruscan alliance to fight the encroachments of the Phocaean Greek colony of Alalia, on the island of Corsica. So Celer Horatius Cocles went along as an observer. The Greek admiral, Callimachus, struck where the immediate effect would be/strongest. His own galley and two more centered in on the Etruscan ship bearing Phipe Camna, the allied admiral, and the older Horatius as observer. As the Etruscans toppled around him, wounded or dead, he realized suddenly that he was no longer a disinterested observer, but a combatant. The Greeks were in no mood for compassion, and had no use for prisoners. Nor had he the time to explain to blood-intoxicated men the niceties of being a military observer, immune to violence. So he went into the fray as a Roman swordsman and emerged the hero of the Etruscan-Carthaginian fleet. When Phipe Camna fell he took over command and with a handful of surviving Etruscan warriors and seamen, held off the three attacking Greek galleys for more than an hour of hand-to-hand combat in which the Greek basileus, Callimachus, died under his sword. As a result of all this, he became hero enough to marry Larthia Camna, niece of the lucumo.''

Kingsley Cusack looked at the other in absolute disbelief. ''Now, how in the hell could the computers, even with a damned Intuitive Computer, know such details?''

His host smiled ruefully. ''I don't know, King. You realize that similar things happen to me in my researches into Cyrus. It's as though you were actually alive, in a different body.''

Kingsley said abruptly, "When can I try it again? I want to get into him when he's somewhat older."

Bryce Norman thought for a while. He said finally, "I'll tell you what, King. I've been at my research into the Persians so hot and heavy that I'm going stale. I figure on taking a couple of weeks off, a very quiet two weeks or so, possibly on one of the new cruise ships into the Caribbean. I'll turn over the key of the apartment to you."

"Fine. When do you leave?"

His friend laughed, in deprecation. "You're really gung-ho, aren't you? I know how you feel and any historian, archeologist, or anthropologist would be the same. I certainly was after my first dream. I wasn't planning on going immediately, but I'll switch my schedule and leave tomorrow. You'll have a full two weeks to research your Horatius at the time of the expulsion of the Tarquins from Rome. But let me give you some warnings."

"Fire away," Kingsley said.

"Don't take more than eight hours at a time, and preferably less, or you'll have worn yourself to a frazzle in two weeks."

Kingsley scowled and said, "Suppose the experience I'm having lasts for longer than eight hours?"

"Then what you do is on your next eight hour dream, the following day, return to the split second following the time you awoke. You can continue this indefinitely. You simply so instruct the dream programmer."

"All right. I've got that."

The academician looked at him unhappily. "There's one thing I must emphatically warn you about, King. It's not wise to use the dreamer frivolously."

"How do you mean?"

"It's one thing, researching the history, particularly since this is your field and you're a serious scholar. It's another thing to use the programmed dreamer machine for entertainment. You can get hooked much easier than you would think."

Kingsley was scowling again. He said, "How do you mean, get hooked?"

His academician friend said, "Just one example. Remember my telling you about the harem of Tamerlane with its couple of hundred ravishingly beautiful women? Well, if you take in something like that, you have a strong tendency to repeat the experience, or to take a crack at some other beauties. In the early days of our research into the machine we had a case of an associate who seemed stable enough and was assigned the equipment. He wound up sleeping with the most beautiful women down through the ages. After about a month of this—we had no idea of what he was doing—he evidently was so enthralled that he no longer took but eight hours at a crack. He began neglecting food, exercise, and even sleep so that he could be with his women. When we discovered him he was in a state of both mental and physical collapse and had to be dragged, screaming, away from the dream programmer."

"That sounds impossible. You said the man was originally stable."

The other shook his head. "No. It's something like the rats with the stimulation wires running to the pleasure centers of their brains. I suppose you've read of the original experiments, many decades ago. If the rats so wired stepped on a little pedal a small charge of electricity went to the pleasure center. They would stand there pressing the pedal over and over again. Nothing else made any difference to them. Food, rest, drink, sex—nor anything else. They would stand there, pressing the pedal until they fell over from exhaustion, dehydration, and starvation."

"Holy smokes," Kingsley said. "But this is a different thing, Bryce."

The academician shook his head. "No, it isn't. And there are things besides sex that you can get hooked on, addicted to. One other chap who early experimented with the dream programmer became addicted to dreams of excitement. Over a period of time he fought as a gladiator in the Roman arena, always winning, of course. He went through the twenty most decisive battles in history, dreaming himself the prevailing general in each one. That is, he was William the Conqueror at Hastings; he was Nelson at Trafalgar; he was Alexander the Great at Arbela, and Cortes at Tenochtitlan. By the time the machine was rescued from him—or him from it—nothing in our present dull society could interest him. Nothing was exciting or even interesting for him any more. He was addicted to the programmed dreams and there was nothing we could do for him. He committed suicide in sheer boredom about a month later."

"Good God," Kingsley Cusack said.

"Yes," the other nodded. "Stick to serious research and you should be all right. Fascinated, but not to the point of becoming addicted."

He took Kingsley back to the dream box and showed

35

him the details of operating it, including the drug which had to be administered by hypodermic immediately before going into the dream world.

Then he gave the younger man a key and said, "I'll be leaving in the morning for my trip. Come in anytime you wish. Let me repeat, all over again, supposedly I am not to allow anyone to utilize this dangerous device, other than myself. My associates have cleared me for it. By no means reveal anything about it and above all don't let anyone else use it. I'm trusting you because I know how much it means to you to acquire your academician's degree, and with the ability to research the Etruscans and early Rome in this manner you should be able to swing it."

Kingsley said simply, "Thanks, Bryce."

"Fine," his older friend told him. "And now clear out. I want to finish off one more dream, the capture of Babylon by Cyrus."

"Have a great trip, Bryce," Kingsley said, and left.

He returned to his own apartment, elated by the whole day. His academician friend was right. Given the use of the dream programmer he would be able to do a work on early Rome that would have the scholastic world at his feet. He wondered why on earth the whole of history was not being so researched. Possibly it was—secretly. Possibly the material learned was being pumped into the data banks without the public being informed. Bryce Norman had made his point about the danger involved in the dream programmer and had mentioned the fact that there was only one in the whole university city of Princeton. On the face of it, whoever was in control was handling the device with rubber gloves. He hadn't asked the academician just who did have jurisdiction over the machine. Possibly it was upper-echelon officials of the International Data Banks Guild.

He spent the balance of the day dictating notes into his vocotyper. While he had shared the brain of young Phipe Horatious Cocles he had shared the boy's memories as well but he was anxious to get down some of the most salient ones as soon as possible. He had no way of knowing how soon some of them might start fading. That was another thing he would have to ask Bryce Norman. Would he retain his artificial memories indefinitely?

In the morning, he impatiently waited until ten o'clock before repairing to his friend's apartment, wanting to give the academician plenty of time to complete packing and to secure reservations for his trip.

But he couldn't hold himself beyond ten. He was impatient to skip forward a few years and check out Horatius as a young man.

The academician was gone by the time he arrived, and he let himself in with the key his friend had provided. He went immediately to the escape sanctum.

All was as it had been the day before. He checked out the dream programmer carefully to make sure he remembered the instructions Bryce Norman had given him. He filled the hypodermic and climbed into the box and began to adjust the electrodes, leaving those that went over his eyes until last.

Chapter Five

Rome—Phipe Horatius Cocles

It was on December seventeenth, the Saturnalia, that for the second time in my life I felt a mind other than my own. I had all but forgotten the time in Caere, when I was but fourteen or fifteen, when it had happened before. It was not distressing, only strange and most difficult to analyze. After a time, I forgot about it, as best I could, and took to enjoying the festival.

The most boisterous of all Roman fetes is that of the Saturnalia, in honor of Saturn, god of seed and sowing. One of the oldest gods of our city, Saturn is the husband of Ops, goddess of fertility, and his temple which stands near the Comitium and next to the temple of Vulcan, contains the city treasury which we call the Saturni Aerarium. During the several days of the Saturnalia, the world, supposedly, is turned upside down. Slaves, though there are not many of these in Rome at this time, became masters, and masters, slaves, so that in every household the owner must obey the orders of his servants. All wore costumes or masks, or both, and the seasonal greeting is Io Saturnalia, and thus Romans salute each other on every occasion. A mock dictator is chosen and called Saturnalicius Princeps and all are subject to his jeering orders. Much wine is drunk, unwatered, and there is music and dancing in the streets and traditionally, since Ops was wife to Saturn, maidens are much more free with their charms than Roman severity permitted for the balance of the year. So, for that matter, are matrons, and many a Roman citizen unknowingly has another's child fathered upon him during the Saturnalia.

All this was probed from my mind within minutes of when the alien presence entered it.

I was attired as a Roman general, though any could see by the youthfulness of my face that I could not possibly have attained that rank. It had been a simple costume to devise, since all that was required was to add to my ordinary spearman's uniform the few signs of rank that distinguish a Roman general from one of his men. High-ranking Romans, unlike Greeks, Carthaginians, and Etruscans, do not make a practice of wearing decorative armor and helmets into battle, which is sensible as such can only attract the attention of the enemy and bring down added missiles on officers whose lives should not be risked during the direction of the combat.

I fancy I cut a handsome figure. I had a cape lined in red, slung in swash fashion over my shoulders and I attempted to strut as I thought a general would strut, and all who passed me who were in actual uniform or in the costume of soldiers, warriors of different countries, or heroes of antiquity, came to the salute. I was having a gay time. Skins or jars of wine were everywhere and the streets teemed with as many women as men and some of them were dressed in a freedom of costume that would have been shocking any other day of the year.

So put up was I by the attention given my high-ranking costume that I took it upon myself to come to the rescue of a masked girl attired in the flimsy down of what was undoubtedly meant to be a water nymph. Her chuckling, half-drunken assailant was a sailor, not of Rome, who had done himself up as best he could to represent a satyr and he was now urging the girl to allow him to embrace her in the fashion that satyrs were traditionally known to embrace nymphs. Ordinarily, such a matter would have drawn only the laughter of all else in the vicinity, and the sailor would have probably gained the kiss and a quick squeeze of a youthful teat which was undoubtedly all he wanted and expected. However, I could see that his face was unshaven and his mouth besmeared with wine and stale vomit. And the girl was obviously still in her middle teens and doubtlessly terrified.

So I strode up to him with a great military air and said, "Satyr, I order you to depart, leaving this nymph to her own choices." It was all meant to be in the best of carnival spirits, but he failed to take it that way. Still holding onto the girl with one begrimed hairy hand, he took a deep swig from his leather bottle and then stared at me through narrowed and wine-shot eyes.

He let go of the wineskin, which was suspended by a leather cord from around his neck, and wiped his mouth partially clean. "Go away, soldier boy," he snickered. "This is men's work." He turned to resume his assault upon the girl.

But then her eyes, through her mask, met mine and there was terror and pleading in them, and the fun was gone out of the situation. "Let go of her," I said flatly, and—an amusing side bit—deep within me I could feel myself thinking, why that's exactly the tone of voice my father, Celer, would have used.

The sailor spun quickly, releasing the girl, and attempted a blow typical of those used by sailors in taverna brawls. However, not for nothing was I a member of the cohort of Valerius. I jabbed my right hand forward, the fingers extended spear-like rather than gathered in a fist, and struck him sharply in that area immediately below the breastbone, the solar plexus. He dropped to the ground like a poled ox, groaning his dismay and then vomiting up the contents of his stomach which proved to be largely wine.

I took the girl by the arm and hurried away, both to spare her the sight of his agony and to avoid any of his friends, if they were among the throng in the vicinity. Not that I was afraid of such but it is not fitting to brawl on the Saturnalia; there are too few days of all-out amusement in Rome.

When we had managed to find a comparatively uncrowded spot near the Vulcanal, the Temple of Vulcan and one of the oldest shrines in Rome, I turned with the intention of telling her that the man had only been drunk and that she would be all right now, but she was looking at me, through her mask, in such manner that it became clear that I would be making a dire mistake if I abandoned this young woman at the present stage of events. Instead, I saluted her pompously, still playing at the general and said, "Fair nymph, I am at your disposal, command me and I obey."

She said, her voice soft and such that a finger seemed to trace faint circles about my chest, "But what did you do to that poor man? You seemed hardly to touch him, and he fell as though dead."

Instinctively, I knew that beneath the mask was a face to match the voice, and I had already ascertained that beneath the thin gown was a woman's body which would be the envy of any true nymph. My mouth was of a sudden dry, and the poise I had maintained until now, bearing out my imposture of a high ranking officer, was difficult to maintain. I had to grip myself to refrain from stuttering in my sudden overwhelming desire not to lose her. "A good general, fair nymph, does not waste his forces. I . . . that is, may I offer you refreshment from one of the street stands?"

She drew her breath in, as though the suggestion was a frightening one. "Oh, but I could never remove my mask in public and I . . . well, I cannot either eat or drink through it."

"Then would you like to continue to stroll?" I said hurriedly, fearing she'd dismiss me. "That is, may I accompany you? Offer you my protection? That is, should we watch the celebration together? Soon the priests will begin the ceremonies before the temple. If we go now, we can find a favorable spot to stand."

She said pettishly, "Oh, I'm tired of priests and their ceremonies. But I shouldn't say that, especially during the fete of Saturn, should I?"

I laughed in deprecation, having regained some of my poise in view of her own naiveté. "The Saturnalia is meant to be enjoyable. If you fail to find enjoyment in watching the sacrifices made by priests, I am sure that

Saturn would rather you do something else." I snapped my fingers as though suddenly inspired. "Before long, the sun will be setting. What say we find a skin of wine, some tidbits of food from the stands and take them to the Capitoline?"

She didn't seem to be opposed, but she said, wonderingly, "Why there? The Capitoline will be practically deserted. Everyone is down here, in celebration."

"For that very reason," I told her triumphantly. I was regaining confidence by the moment. "The workingmen will all be gone from the construction of the Capitoline Triad Temple and we can find a spot to sit and watch the sunset and the crowds beneath and there you will be able to remove your mask and sip our wine and taste the specialties of the day."

"Ah," she mocked. "Now I see your scheme. You wish to have me remove my mask."

I saluted her, once more the general. "Fair nymph, I deny it not."

She laughed a tinkling, most disturbing laugh, and we were off to find the wine and picnic lunch, which, of course, was no problem during the Saturnalia since the streets were one big market of sweets, wines, breads, cheeses, meats, and fruit.

We took the Clivus Capitolinus, which is the western extention of the Sacred Way and mounts from the Forum to the top of the Capitoline hill. I had been right. In a nook, on the steps of the soon-to-be-completed temple, we found a spot where we could remain undetected by the very few who were in the vicinity—most of these were on similar mission to our own—and could look out over the celebrants crowded in the Forum and the green slopes of the Palatine to the right. Below us was the Temple of Saturn, and there the crowds were particularly dense as the priests, bareheaded on this occasion, performed the ritual, headed by Tarquin Superbus himself in his aspect of Pontus Maximus.

And now I could wait no longer. I lifted my hands to remove her mask, nor did she ought to stay me; but when her face was revealed she looked into my eyes with a touch of anxiety, before shifting her own eyes and saying lowly, "Do you still call me fair nymph?" Her fingers twisted a pleat of her robe.

Except for her voice, which had a quality to be expected only in an older and experienced woman, she was hardly more than a child. In fact, my eyes involuntarily went down to her bosom, but the swell of her breasts proclaimed her maturity. Her eyes were soft, as her voice was soft, and her features were even and classical, although there was an elfin touch about the corners of her mouth so that they went down at the slightest suggestion of humor. Her hair was golden, neither blond nor brunette but as though of very delicate honey, and her mouth was full and soft, as a woman's mouth, eternal woman.

"Instead, fair goddess," I told her. I reached out my hands and took her shoulders and brought her closer to me and pressed my mouth to hers. Her eyes widened and her body tensed, but she did not resist me. Her kiss had a quality of a child's kiss, but still, impossibly, that of a full woman.

When I released her, she looked at me wonderingly. "That is the first time a man other than my father has kissed me," she said.

I scoffed. "A likely tale."

She was hurt and looked away and began fumbling among the things we had bought. "It is true," she said lowly. And I knew it was, and was ashamed.

We sat and drank our wine and ate our bread and meat and watched the crowds below, though not as much as we watched each other. "My name is Phipe Horatius," I said finally.

"Horatius?" she said. "The Horatians are one of the proudest gentes of Rome. Of what family, Phipe?"

"Cocles. If you look carefully, you can see the entrance to my home there on the corner of the Palatine."

"Cocles?" she said, distressed. "But then you are a plebian."

I said stiffly, "And does that make so much difference to you?"

Instead of answering, she said, "You may call me Carmenta."

I said, still stiffly, "And of what family of the Carmentian gens, may I ask? It is certainly one of the most numerous in the city."

"That," she said evasively, "must remain my secret, though I am surprised that you have not recognized my face."

"You need not be," I told her glumly. "Although I am a citizen, I've spent little time in Rome and am poorly acquainted."

"Then you must belong to one of the rural gentes . . . but no, you said your home was on the Palantine." And then my name came to her. "Phipe Horatius. Why you are the young man who accompanied Celer Horatius to Cumae to procure the Sibyl-line Books.''

"Yes, I have made several trips with my father, when he has gone on embassy. I must assume," I said unhappily, "that you are of patrician family."

She looked down at her feet, which were shod Etrus-can style with up-pointed toes and straps behind the heels and up over the ankles. They were expensive shoes and seen only on the feet of the more wealthy Roman women. She nodded, unhappy too.

"And hence," I pressed on. "I would not be wel-come in your home. Nor my father, if he came to consult your parents."

She bit her lower lip and said suddenly, "It is Satur-nalia, and the world is turned upside down. Let us return to our food and . . . and, if you will, you may . . . do that again to me."

And suddenly nothing made any difference but that she was woman and I was man, and when I kissed her I put the palm of my hand over her right breast and caressed it gently as our lips met. She sighed into my mouth, instinctively knowledgeable about the working of lips and ignoring the fondling of my hand—or perhaps assumed that such always was the practice when a maid and a man pressed mouths together.

In youth, there is no limit of time that can be spent at kissing and petting and we sat there for hours and played at love. And though she allowed me the freedom of her bosom, and even to stroke her rounded hips and buttocks, and indeed the silken softness of her inner thighs and the mystery of the shrine of the vulva where they meet, still she would not grant me the ultimate favor though I was by this time raging in my masculine need.

It was fully dark by the time, hand in hand, we led each other down the flint pavement of the Clivius Capitolinus and though the activities were continuing and would continue until dawn, the crowd was already beginning to thin. I had assumed that she would allow me to escort her to her home, or at least to its vicinity and thus I would be able to question a passerby and find her full name. But she would not have it that way, insisting that I leave her at the Temple of Vulcan and pledge my honor to make no attempt whatsoever to discover her identity.

"Only," I said, "if you will pledge your own word to meet me here again tomorrow."

And that she did. I stood and watched after her, her mask on her face again, as she disappeared into the crowd of revelers who were fast becoming reeling drunk after this long day of festivity.

Chapter Six

Princeton—Kingsley Cusack

Kingsley Cusack came back into the present and for a moment remained in the dream programmer box breathing deeply. He wondered if someone who had dreamed as often as Bryce Norman ever got so used to it that it didn't have the psychic effect that it gave himself. There was no two ways about it. It wrung you out psychologically.

He detached the electrodes and swung himself out of the box. He went over to the academician's desk and sat down in his swivel chair to gather his thoughts. He had requested a full eight hours. He brought his transceiver from his inner jacket pocket, flicked the cover back and pressed the time stud. It was a little after six o'clock.

In actuality, he was mildly disappointed. He had requested of the dream programmer eight hours in the mind of Horatius when he was a young man and in Rome. And that's what he had gotten. However, most of the time was spent in the company of a young woman, sitting and picnicking, and later necking, in a remote spot. He had hoped to see a good deal of Rome through the young Roman's eyes.

Of course, he had seen the Capitoline Triad Temple, still abuilding, and quite a bit of the Forum, and he had gone up the Sacred Way. He had also witnessed at least part of a Saturnalia, which was something, at least. He wondered if any other contemporary had ever witnessed that all-out Roman festival. Most likely, or, at least, possibly.

He had wondered before if all history was being investigated by those who had access to the machine. But now that he thought about it, he doubted it. All history covered a tremendous span, and while you were dreaming time passed at the same pace as it did in the real world. If you spent six months of your life crossing and recrossing the Atlantic with Columbus, that would be six months of your real life gone by.

His academician friend was an example. Bryce Norman was evidently throughly investigating the early Persians. It would possibly take him years to do the job, particularly since he allowed himself only eight hours out of the twenty-four. And possibly not even that much, since he must take some time out to collate his notes.

Which reminded Kingsley that he should get to his own notes. The day was already well advanced and he wanted to get onto his vocotyper and at least dictate some descriptions of such things as the Vulcanal Temple, the Temple of Saturn, and Tarquin Superbus in his role of Pontus Maximus, though he had seen the rex only from a distance.

He got to his feet and prepared to leave, casting a

longing look at the dream programmer. He would love to take on another eight hours. After all, he had only two weeks, and he suspected that when Bryce Norman returned he would take over the equipment to the point where Kingsley would have little access to it. Not that he blamed his friend. He could see that if you had the device it would be best to have it continually available. You might be taking notes and come to a point where you wanted some small detail, and take a dream that lasted but five or ten minutes to get it.

But he shook his head. If he took another programmed dream now it would be two o'clock in the morning before he came out of it. And his friend had been emphatic about the dangers of overdoing. He needed real sleep, he needed exercise, and he needed food. Which reminded him. He hadn't eaten lunch and it was nearly his dinner time. He didn't feel hungry since he was still keyed up, but he knew he was going to have to eat.

He started toward the door and was in the living room when the identity screen buzzed. He didn't have the vaguest idea who it might be. He went over to Bryce Norman's living room desk and pressed the identity screen button and looked at the door. He didn't recognize the face. It certainly didn't look like a student or a faculty member.

And then, to his surprise, he heard what seemed to be a key in the lock. He strode over quickly and flung the door open. There were two men, one of whom was hurriedly putting his hand in a pocket. Kingsley scowled. Had the man actually been unlocking the door and hidden the key when he'd heard Kingsley coming.

He couldn't imagine the academician giving another key to someone.

And particularly to these two. They were rather heavyset men, probably in their midthirties, with darkish complexions. They were dressed a bit more flamboyantly than was usual in the university city; they both wore hats, which was unusual in Princeton.

Kingsley said, "What can I do for you?"

On the face of it, they were surprised to see him.

The one closest to Kingsley growled, "Who in the hell are you?" He tried to peer past him into the living room.

Kingsley said, "I'm Doctor Kingsley Cusack." He knew very well now that the man had nothing to do with the university. His voice indicated that he had acquired only a minimum of education. "The academician is away, I am afraid."

"Well, what are you doing here?"

"Really now," Kingsley said, irritated by the man's brusque directness. "The academician has given me permission to have the run of his apartment while he's on vacation. What possible business is it of yours?"

"Kind of baby sitting it, eh?"

"Not exactly, but call it that, if you wish. Now just what is it you want?"

Both of the two looked frustrated.

The one in the rear muttered to the one who had so far done all the talking, "We better check it out with the boss."

The other said, "Yeah, I guess so." And then to Kingsley, "Our business is with Norman. How long did you say he was going to be off?"

51

"I didn't," Kingsley said testily. "But he was expecting to be away for two weeks, starting today. I suggest that you return at that time."

The other was unhappy. He rubbed the end of his nose with a forefinger, before saying, "Look, do you mind if we come in and look around?"

"Certainly I mind," Kingsley said indignantly. "I don't know either of you."

"Okay," the stranger sighed. "Maybe we'll see you later, chum-pal."

The two turned and made off down the hall.

Kingsley Cusack stared after them, wondering how in the world they had gotten into the elevators of the Longfellow Building. It should have been impossible. There would be no problem entering the lobby on the ground floor: Anyone could do that. But the elevators all had identity screens. If you were a resident, your face was in the data banks and you were automatically checked and passed. But if you were a visitor, you had to identify yourself and report where you were going. The computers then checked with the resident of the apartment which was your destination and passed you if you were okayed.

But how had these two gotten up here? Kingsley shrugged. He waited until he felt the pair would be gone from the hall before leaving. They had evidently gotten the impression that he was staying in the academician's digs on a full-time basis, and he didn't want them to think otherwise. They might return while he was away and go about whatever it was they had in mind. He was still of the opinion that they had been attempting to open the door when he confronted them.

He went down to his own apartment and treated himself to a stiff drink before going into his small dining room to dial a meal.

For some reason he couldn't put his finger upon, his apartment seemed sterile to him, unlived in. He had never felt that way before. He was a confirmed bachelor, and although he'd had his quota of women in his time, it had never occurred to him to take up a permanent relationship with any of them. In fact, he soon became more or less impatient if one of his quick rolls in the hay developed into the girl's staying more than one night in his apartment.

As he sat at the table, finishing the drink and waiting for the delivery of whale steak, vegetables, and salad, his mind went back to Carmenta. God, but she was, or at least had been, a pretty, shapely thing. From what he had seen of the other Roman women at the Saturnalia, she must have been an exception with her honey-blonde hair.

He had experienced everything that young Horatius had experienced, in the kissing and fondling of the girl, in the feeling of her rounded body against the Roman's chest. And for a moment he felt a pang of envy of the other.

But that was ridiculous. Phipe Horatius Cocles didn't exist, and even, possibly, never had. He was a figment of the dream programmer's skill.

The food came and he ate it hurriedly, wanting to get on with his notes. Bryce had told him that he must get exercise and plenty of real sleep, but this was the first day and exercise could wait. And he decided that he would devote exactly five hours a night to sleep, although usually he took a full eight. Five hours would be enough; and with eight hours in the dream box he would have eleven hours for exercise, meals, and his notes and studies. He decided that he would spend one hour a day, out in the park, exercising furiously. That should be enough. It was only for two weeks, and he was in good physical condition after Yucatan.

He finished the meal impatiently, put the dirty dishes and utensils back on the center of the table and pressed the stud which would return them to the basements and the automated kitchen equipment there.

He went on back into his living-room-cum-library-and-study, dialed himself a long glass of ale and seated himself before his vocotyper in satisfaction. When he had finished with the description of the Saturnalia and his eight hours in Rome, he went on into the memories he had picked up in the mind of Horatius.

In actuality, he didn't get the five hours of sleep that he had alloted to himself for that night. His mind was in too much of a turmoil. He was trying to figure out just what period of Horatius' life he wanted to dip into next. After all, he had only two weeks: fourteen days, with eight hours of dreaming in each. One hundred and twelve hours in all. A little more than four and a half days. Not very much time in which to investigate a man's full life.

Kingsley finally fell off to sleep and was up bright and early at dawn. He went up to the academician's apartment after he had eaten a hurried breakfast; but before going into the sanctum he looked about to see if there were any signs of the two strangers' having returned and forced entrance. There didn't seem to be.

He went on into the escape sanctum and went through the same motions he had the previous day: at the very last, plunging the hypodermic into his arm.

Chapter Seven

Vicinity of Tibur—Phipe Horatius Cocles

The cohort of Marcus Valerius was on the march to relieve the town of Tibur when for the third time the strange alien mind entered mine. This time it came as less of a surprise. The first occurrence, when I had been a student, the feeling lasted but an hour or two; the second time it continued for some eight hours, there at the Saturnalia where I met Carmenta. I had no way of knowing how long I would be possessed this time. However, I brought my own mind back to the present.

We were being sent out against a war band of Etruscans who had drifted down from Perugia and were raiding in an area near Tibur, a town originally founded by the Siculi, centuries before Rome had begun, but now under our domination.

Rome was not at war with Perugia, one of the twelve cities of the Etruscan Confederation, nor by Etruscan usage was this raiding expedition to be held against the officials of that city. And to understand this it is necessary to realize the Etruscan attitude toward armed conflict. They believe that there can be three types of war: a private affair, a national one involving any of the individual city-states, or, most rare of all, one involving the whole Etruscan Confederation.

If an individual Etruscan chief wishes to, and can, gather about him a force of adventurers large enough to launch an expedition for the purpose of seizing booty, avenging a former attack against his interests, or continuing a blood feud, it is not usually considered a matter of business of the lucumo and the senate of the city from which he originates. He is going forth, as did the Greek warriors of which Homer sang, on a personal campaign, a private matter. If he is victorious, he and his men retain what loot they have collected; if his force is decimated, the city from which he came takes no action. This type of warfare is the most common of all in Etruria, taking place on both land and sea, for the Etruscans are sometimes pirates as well as raiders.

National wars are another matter. Each Etruscan city has its fetiales whose office is sacred and whose persons are inviolate when they are performing their duties. In case of a dispute between an Etruscan city and an alien one, a delegation of fetiales is sent to the aggrieving town to present the case before the senate. They wear special ceremonial clothing and usually ride in chariots while on a mission. They state their version of the matter with dignity, rather than in an aggressive tone, and request that it be handled in due haste, usually within ten days. If the offending city refuses their demands, they return home and inform their own senate that war is called for. If their senate so decides, the fetiales return to the country of the enemy and cast a spear, iron tipped, into the enemy's territory. The war is then on, and the Etruscan city is committed as a whole. The armed forces go forth, led by the lucumo and marshalled according to gens so that relative will be fighting next to relative, supporting each other and trying to excel in each other's eyes.

A war in which the Etruscan Confederation as a whole participates is rare indeed, since the league they form is not a military one but largely religious and it is seldom that the individual interests of all twelve cities so coincide that they consider concerted action. In fact, I can think of but one such case. If such a war were to be decided upon, the decision would be made at the annual gathering of the lucumones at the Temple of Voltumna. It would be necessary to appoint a lar to be head of all the hosts and it would be his task, and not a simple one, for the Etruscans are the greatest individualists in the world, to summon a host to carry out the desires of the conference.

The group, then, against which we were marching, belonged to the first category. That is, they were a private force, probably composed largely of younger warriors grown bored with the routine of daily life. They had rallied around some Perugian chief who felt the same and who desired to add both to the luster of his name and to his property. The band had evidently been on its good behavior as it trekked across the territory of such intervening Etruscan cities as Chiusi, Orvieto, and Falerii, but now that it had penetrated Latium they began pillaging the villages, rounding up the cattle and in general making thieving nuisances of themselves. Tarquin Superbus, no more than irritated by such minor military matters, dispatched Marcus Valerius to the scene with orders to make an example of this band of robbers. Rome should have a reputation strong enough that pirates and bandits would avoid trouble with the city of the seven hills.

The town of Tibur, not quite large enough to be called a city, lies at the end of the valley of the Aniene on the lower slopes of the Sabine hills. It is spectacularly located overlooking the Roman Campagna, the river so looping around the town that it borders it on three sides, and the cascades are famed. When our cohort arrived, we found that the citizens had withdrawn behind the walls and were watching with wan faces the smoke going up from their homes along the slopes. Valerius had no need to ask where the raiders had been reported last. Where the smoke pillars were thickest would be the focal point of the enemy forces.

We had a soldier's meal and then rested for a short time, all the whole during which Valerius was being harassed by the town fathers to hasten. He knew better, as an old campaigner, than to fight his men with empty stomachs and weary from a long, fast march. However, soon enough we were up again and tramping down the hills toward the foe.

Beside me, Titius Herminius grinned sourly, and there was an element of mockery in his voice when he said from the side of his mouth, "Nervous, Horatius?" He'd been in the cohort for over a year and had proven himself on more than one occasion.

"Of course," I growled back.

He was evidently surprised that I admitted it, probably considering that it was below a Roman spearman's pride to admit nervousness in the face of combat. Let him think what he wanted, no man goes into mortal fray for the first time without a twinge of fear and cold sweat sticking shirt to back.

"Silence in the ranks!" a junior officer bawled. "Save your breath for the Tuscans, you'll need it."

The Etruscans had mounted scouts about, and we had been spotted even before we marched into Tibur. Now they kept an eye on us as we proceeded down the road. I was inwardly worried about the fact that at least some of them were mounted while we were on foot. They were going to be able to avoid us if they wished, or hang on our flanks and harass us with bows or slings. It hadn't occurred to me that they had accumulated considerable booty and had no intention of giving it up, and while they might be mounted, the ox-drawn carts which contained their loot were slow moving indeed.

When we came up on them, it became obvious that they intended to fight. Only about a third were mounted on horseback. There were also six or eight two-man chariots which we Romans no longer use in battle, but the rest were footmen. I would estimate that we were equal in numbers. They were deployed in line with their baggage to the rear. There was a good deal of this, possibly thirty wagons and carts. No wonder they were determined to fight. If they could take this amount of loot home, their raid would have been a success indeed and they themselves the envy of the other young warriors of Perugia. For young they were. I doubt if any of them had reached the age of twnety-five. It is youth that goes seeking trouble.

Valerius snapped, "Open phalanx!" And we deployed from our line of march to face the ranks of the Perugian raiders. We were six deep, the men in the rear armed with pikes considerably longer than those in the front rank, whose weapons were but six feet in length. Besides these pikes, each man had a javelin which was usually thrown immediately before the enemy was engaged hand-to-hand. As opposed to tight phalanx order, we now stood with two yards between each man so that the pikes from behind could reach through and to give sufficient room to use our weapons and maneuver. The officers stood immediately behind, their eyes seeking out the slightest deviation from the line, snarling out commands to keep us in perfect dress.

In a moment, I expected Valerius' command to advance against the enemy, but at that point a chariot came charging out before the ranks of the Etruscan raiders, churning up dust and gravel, and dashed toward us. It came to a halt fifty feet or so before our hedge of spears and a magnificently armored warrior jumped to the ground with a clash of arms and armor. He could have been taken from the illustration on a well-done Grecian vase imported from Attica and ornamented with some scene of the doings of gods and heroes. His shield was round and studded with ornament, his breastplate was engraved, his brazen greaves were highly polished, and his helmet haughtily bore a black horse plume which gave him an additional full foot of seeming height.

He brandished his sword toward us and called out in boastful scorn in the old tongue, the sacred tongue of the Etruscans, "I am Mutius of Perugia, warchief of the Precu gens and commander of this band and challenge to personal combat a chief of equal rank!"

The Etruscan footmen beat fiercely with their swords upon their shields in approval of the duel and the bravery of their chief. It set up a din so that I could scarce hear my own commander, Valerius, who rasped at me, "Horatius, what did he say in this bastard language?"

I said, "Sir, he is the chief of the raiders and challenges you to personal combat."

Valerius snorted and said brittily, "Titius Herminius, can you bring that Tuscan down?"

Titius Herminius was noted as our best javelin man. He eyed the strutting Etruscan and shook his head. "No, sir. If he came another ten feet forward, yes sir."

I said, and there must have been an edge of horrified disbelief in my voice, "Sir, it is a custom of the Etruscans. He challanges you to honorable man-to-man combat."

Our commander cast a bleak look at me. "Silence, spearman, or tonight you are flogged to ribbons. Dress up, your pike is a full two inches low!"

The Etruscan had come nearer, still shaking his sword in defiance. He evidently had decided that none among us had understood the challenge in the old tongue. His everyday language was undoubtedly Umbrian, but he called now in miserable Latin, "I am Mutius Precu, chief of this band and challenge your leader to personal combat!" And behind him his men again signalled their approval with a clamorous banging of their shields.

But the Perugian chief was now within range. Valerius rasped, "Titius Herminius! Bring him down!"

With a fluid but powerful cast, Herminius loosed his javelin and it sped with all the precision of perfect aim. The Etruscan, in midstride, looked up in surprise and found insufficient time to bring his shield to his defense. The javelin pierced him immediately below the breastplate, going completely through his body so that the head projected from behind. He turned slowly and with a strange dignity and crumbled to the ground, his gorgeous arms and armor clanging as they had when he had so bravely leapt from his chariot.

With an enraged roar, the Etruscan line exploded toward us, chariots and horsemen leading.

As though we were on parade, his voice even and harsh, Valerius called, "First-rank javelins to be devoted to horses and chariots. Second- and third-rank javelins to be devoted to cavalry." He paused a moment, then as the chariots rapidly narrowed the distance between us, called, "First rank javelins, throw!"

He was aware of the fact that the chariots probably bore the officers or outstanding warriors of the enemy and hence had assigned them a greater number of our missiles than should ordinarily be called for against so small a number. As it was, the six chariots went down in a screaming, kicking, thrashing confusion of horses and of impaled or crushed men. I saw only two or three of the occupants roll free, and behind them the Etruscan cavalry pounded, so that they would be lucky to escape death under the hoofs.

Only one of the vehicles got through to our ranks and plunged into our pikes. For a moment, it seemed as though the phalanx had been broken and that the horsemen and the footmen charging behind would wedge into the opening and break our wall of men into fragments to be dealt with individually. But no, the voices of our officers barked out, "Close ranks, close ranks! Dress your line!" And we struggled and pushed back together so that again we presented a perfect hedge of spear points. The chariot, both of its occupants dead, was allowed to pass on through and its pain maddened-horses plunged across the field.

By the time the horse arrived, their first edge of anger must have been blunted to the point that they realized that impaling themselves on our Roman pikes was not going to avenge their fallen leader, so they began to vear off to right and left, dispatching arrows and javelins at us in great number.

Valerius, "Second- and third-rank javelins, throw!" And the volley hit the horsemen just as they were trying to break away, leaving the immediate charge to the spearmen who followed. Horses and riders went down, but not in nearly so devastating a manner as the chariot charge had been met. They were probably going to attempt to flank, but for the moment Valerius paid no heed to that. The enemy line of spearmen was about to crash into us. Behind them the Etruscan trumpets, a musical instrument they had invented, were pealing their shrill war notes, hysterically.

They advanced in good order, considering that they were coming in on a run, and most of them bore the Etruscan pike called the hasta. They took heavy casualties from the javelins of our fourth, fifth, and sixth lines, when they were no more than ten paces off, but were slowed not at all.

We stood firm and took the charge and for a moment so hard was the initial impact that we were pushed backward. Those in the front rank were shield to shield with the foe, their spearpoints either high in the air, down to the ground, or wedged between shields to press against men or metal somewhere in the thick of humanity.

But we held, though at this point we took casualties. Our six deep ranks were too much for the raider warriors who had hit us only three ranks deep. We outweighed them, and in only moments they broke away. I could hear Valerius shouting, "Fifth and sixth ranks, about-face! Forward four paces! Sixth rank, kneel!"

The cavalry had sped around our flanks and was attempting to catch us from the rear. Our sixth rank dropped to one knee, put the bottom edge of their shields to the ground, and then grounded their pikes, elevating the points and bracing the butts. The fifth and sixth ranks now presented a formidable defense to our mounted foe, and they sheered off again, throwing a score or so javelins as they went.

And now the enemy began to pull back to reorganize. It was not the Etruscan way to go on the defensive, far to the contrary. And I noticed the difference between our two peoples. The Romans had received their charge grimly, stubbornly, fighting exactly as commanded and with hardly a budge in the ranks. The Etruscans, to the contrary, came in with great excitement, shouting war cries, singing war songs, and sometimes laughing in sheer exuberation.

But they must have decided now that a pellmell charge against our close-knit phalanx was suicide and that it must be broken by some other method. They realized that we were without auxiliaries such as would ordinarily accompany a cohort of Roman troops, and thus without slingers or archers. Consequently, they stood off from us, both horse and foot, and began firing arrows and occasionally riding close enough to dispatch a javelin. Several of our men fell.

Valerius bit out gruffly, "Tight phalanx!" And moving in perfect order, we stepped closer together. The first rank knelt, shield to the ground, pike advanced, shield linked to that of the neighbor to each side. The second rank placed their shields up atop those of the first rank, which brought them higher than eye level. Those behind held their shields above their heads, forming a roof. We were a closed fortress of metal and the arrows and javelins fell without effect.

But Valerius must have decided that the enemy was most likely in a state of confusion, having lost not only the chief of the band but probably most of its officers as well. He decided to strike before they could reorganize themselves. So after suffering without losses their javelins and arrows for a short time, we reformed again in open phalanx and at the double advanced toward the ox carts and wagons which contained the Etruscan loot and which had been held in the rear of their forces.

It was now either do or die for them. If their booty was captured and they had to return to Perugia with nothing to show for their expedition but their casualties, they would have been defeated indeed. Nor was there any chance of the baggage train escaping us, since nothing moves so slowly as oxen pulling heavy wagons.

No, the only thing for it was to meet us again, and

this time they must have decided to succeed or go down to a man. While we were still advancing on the double, the remainder of their horse came galloping at us, and we didn't see their strategy until the last moment, when they suddenly formed a wedge and hit our line at full tilt and with such force that although the first twenty or so horses and men went down to black death on the points of our spears, the phalanx was broken and some of the horsemen galloped all the way through and out behind.

The enemy spearmen now headed for our center, where the line had been crashed by their horse, screaming their battle cries and obviously feeling that at last they would get through our inpenetrable hedge of spears and meet us hand-to-hand. But Valerius and his officers were unfazed, continually shouting, "Close ranks, close ranks! Dress your lines!" And sometimes, right in the thickest crush of the fighting and incongruously, considering the situation, one of these Roman veterans would call out, "Larthius, your shield is two inches high. Horatius, you are half a foot behind. Dress it up!"

The cavalry had largely spent itself in that desperate attack, for horsemen should not charge competent spearmen; and the fight was now between us foot. And although the Etruscans came in bravely and tried to exploit the break in the phalanx that their horse had sacrificed themselves to make, they lacked the numbers to defeat us. In surprisingly short order they had ceased to exist as a unit and the fighting was through except for cleaning up.

Valerius shouted orders for us to break into squads and the phalanx, for the first time, dissolved as such, and each squad under its own officer or sergeant took up the pursuit of the raiders. Their cavalry, of course, evaded us, and possibly a hundred or so of the footmen, who escaped as best they could and attempted to return to their own land through country they had pillaged while in strength. I doubt if many of them could escape vengeful farmers who must have sought them out of their hiding places and killed them with farm implements; a terrible way for a warrior to meet his end.

Needless to say, we retrieved practically all of the plunder with the intentions of later returning it to Tibur and putting it into the hands of the town fathers so that they could assume the task of restoring the property to rightful owners. Some of us might have looked at the great pile of loot with longing, thinking that we, as the conquerors, should have at least a portion of the booty; but Rome is ruled by law and Roman soldiers do not plunder within the boundries of the lands of allies.

Strangely enough, it was after the collapse of the raiding party as a whole that our cohort took the most losses. Fighting in small groups, and even as individuals, the Etruscan warriors were at least as competent as ourselves. In the phalanx and acting in unison under the commands of our veterans and especially Valerius, we were more than a match for them; but now, in small units, we had to fight it out man for man to clean them up, and though we outnumbered them heavily, they most often refused to surrender.

It was at this time that, so far as I can be certain, I killed my first man. For in the ranks I had thrown my javelin, but failed to see whether it had struck its mark. And in the melee I had thrust with my pike as strongly as Herminius who stood at my right, but was unable to be sure that its point ever did more than wound the warrior who pressed against me. But now, in the open, with the raiders scattered, I found myself face-to-face with a panting warrior who had lost his helmet and was bespattered with blood and dirt but was still defiantly holding sword and shield ready.

"Now yield," I demanded of him. Small quarter was being given by my companions, but, after all, I was half-Etruscan myself and did not wish to kill the man unnecessarily.

He grinned at me and shook his head. "Look about you, Roman," he chuckled in deprecation. "The others are not taking prisoners, and why should they? If you return with us to Rome, as prisoners, we could never be slaves. Etruscans make poor slaves, Roman, as all men know. Besides, in time Tarquin would probably set us free, and your chief knows it, and since he is a Roman and thinks as Romans do, he would rather finish us now than take the chance of fighting us again. Were I to surrender to you, I suspect my throat would be cut within the hour. So defend yourself, Roman, it is you or me."

And with that, and with excitement aglow in his weary face, he rushed me. Tired as I was from the long battle and the marching and maneuvering, I was still not so exhausted as he. Besides, I had a double advantage, for I knew well the Etruscan sword drill, having studied under competent veterans in Caere, and could foresee his every blow before he made it. But he did not understand our Roman methods of infighting, and fell a victim to my third feint. It is not a pleasure to slay your first man, even though he be a raider devastating the countryside of your people, and I walked away from his body with mingled emotions. He had died well, laughter in his eyes even as they went dull and he looked upon black death. I could not but wonder if I would so face the hereafter, if there be a hereafter.

That night as we squatted about our fires, gorging ourselves with roast goat and mutton, for Valerius had at least allowed us to butcher some of the livestock which we had freed from the raiders, I was confronted by our commander who came up to the fireside where I chewed industriously at my meat beside Titius Herminius and others of my squad comrades.

Marcus Valerius looked down upon me, motioning to us all not to stand to attention and his face was characteristically bleak. "Horatius," he said, "tell me again of the Tuscan challenge to personal combat."

Although he had put us at our ease, I came to my feet and looked into his face, the better to communicate. I said, "It is an Etruscan custom. In warfare one of their chiefs will challenge another of equal rank to meet him. It is a sign of high courage and greatly approved of by the Etruscan footmen. I understand that on some occasions the battle is decided in such way. That side whose chief is defeated leaves the field to the other force."

Valerius was not a laughing man, indeed he was ever cold, gray, and grim, but now his mouth twisted in bleak humor. "Horatius, you are a Roman, and consequently follow the Roman way. You are, further, a soldier, not a warrior. Warriors sometimes become heroes. Soldiers remain soldiers. Their task is to kill the enemies of Rome, win battles against the foes of

Rome, not to become heroes.'' He grunted. "Resume your meal, Horatius.''

He looked at Herminius and the other spearmen about the fire and said, ''That meat looks good, give me a portion, spearman.'' And with that he squatted down to join us, gnawing on a barbequed kid's hind quarters like the rest. Although a patrician born, as an old campaigner Marcus Valerius knew well the ways of the trooper and knew as well when it was time to unbend and become a comrade of the men he led so strictly in battle.

After a few minutes of eating, he shook the bone at me and went back to his point. ''You saw what happened to the Perugians, as a result of the arrogance and supposed bravery of their strutting commander who evidently thought himself as another Menelaus or Ajax. He died and then they were without their war chief. In blind fury—a state no true soldier should ever allow himself to get into—the remaining leaders charged in their chariots, and were cut down to a man. By the time the battle was really joined, there was probably not an officer left among them.''

He tore another bite from his goat bone before resuming, his mouth full. ''We lost perhaps thirty soldiers, Horatius, but we destroyed five hundred warriors who were not adverse to raiding Roman territory and hence could be expected to do it again some time in the future, had they lived. They were enemies of Rome and we destroyed them as we must destroy all enemies of Rome. Had I dashed out, upon our friend's challenge, our friend Mutius Precu, to play Hector to his Achilles, I might well have fallen, for none will gainsay the valor of the Tuscans. Then what might have happened, Horatius? Without its veteran captain, might not the cohort have fallen to the onslaught of the enemy? Let us go further. Our cohort defeated, might not the Perugians have stormed the walls of Tibur and captured the town we had been sent to defend? Let us go still further. When these victorious Tuscans had returned home, laughing and rich with their victory and spoil, would not they have bragged how easy it was to defeat Roman arms and to sack Roman towns? And how many future expeditions from not only Perugian, but other Tuscan cities as well, would not come down upon us next season?''

I said uncomfortably, ''The Etruscans are our allies, not our foes. Why, even our rex, Tarquin, is of Etruscan descent.''

Valerius said, the red fire glittering in his eyes, ''Rome has had various reges, Horatius, and some were Latin and some Sabine and some Tuscan. And we have fought various enemies in the short history of Rome and some were Latin and some Sabine and some Tuscan. For though we are of many races, we are a strange amalgamation. What we must keep ever in mind is that we are Roman, no matter what our many racial origins. And the enemies of Rome must be destroyed if our city's destiny is to be fulfilled.'' He said the last in a harsh tone, which brought a heavy murmur of approval from the various footmen who had drifted up to hear the discussion.

Titius Herminius, from around his food, growled, ''Right!''

But inwardly I was strangely affected. There was a

chauvinism abuilding in Rome stronger than any before. Others might love their city to the point where they would give their all for its sake, so far as property or even life was concerned. But I could not think of such men as Astur the Etruscan or Mamilius the Latin surrendering all sense of honor, all ethics, all mores, for the defense of Volterra or Tusculum. However, I could feel that Marcus Valerius or Titius Herminius, yes, or my father, Celer Horatius, would do just that for Rome did the need arise. Perhaps in his code of honor my father might have fallen on his sword afterwards, did it become necessary to betray even close friends, such as those of Caere, for the sake of Rome's destiny, but betray them he would, I felt sure, if Rome demanded. Aye! I felt greatly twisted within.

Chapter Eight

Princeton—Kingsley Cusack

Once again, after awakening, Kingsley sat in the academician's swivel chair to regain control of himself. Wars were a thing of the past in this modern age of the United States of the Americas. There hadn't been one in his memory. The only weapons he had ever handled had been museum pieces. He had never even fired a hunting rifle in his life.

He let air out of his lungs with a whoosh. Now he had the clearest memories of his killing men with spear and sword. He had the memories of blood and gore and of the light of life going out of a man's eyes as he bled to death.

Well, if he had chosen a Roman warrior of old with whom to identify in his programmed dreams, he must expect such matters. The overthrow of the Tarquins had not been accomplished without bloodshed.

He took out his transceiver and checked the time and decided to eat before getting to his notes.

On his way back to his own apartment, he changed

his mind about taking his meal in his own quarters and decided to go down to one of the Longfellow Building's restaurants, just for a change. He'd be going stale if he spent all of his hours in his apartment and that of Bryce Norman, and he hadn't been anywhere else since his return from Yucatan.

He decided to make it the Balkan Room, which was on the second floor along with various other restaurants, bars, and nightspots.

The place was only moderately full at this time of day, and he had no difficulty in finding an unoccupied table.

He studied the menu set in the table top and decided to eat Hungarian. He ordered halaszle, Hungary's answer to bouillabaisse, paprikas, a veal stew sprinkled with clotted cream, and, for dessert, retes, the Hungarian strudel. He decided upon a half-bottle of dry Szamorodni. He could have ordered any of the dishes in his own apartment, of course, but he rather liked the Eastern European decor here; and also the hum of voices and the faint Balkan music in the background were a welcome change.

He waited a bit impatiently for the food to come. He wanted to get to his notes. That battle scene and the memories of Horatius he had acquired dealing with the war methods of the Romans and Etruscans were priceless to his research.

A voice said, "Do you mind if I share your table?"

He looked up, somewhat surprised. The place wasn't as packed as all that. However, the girl was pretty in a fey sort of way. Olive complexion, sparkling dark eyes, and a very full red mouth, which surprised Kingsley. Few of the students utilized cosmetics anymore. They weren't an in-thing in this age of liberated women. Her hair—worn shoulder length, which was also somewhat passé—was so black it seemed to be dyed; but no, it had too much natural sheen for that. She was dressed simply in a black turtleneck sweater and black Bermuda shorts, which effectively showed off her good figure.

He said, half-rising, "Of course not."

She said, and her voice went with face and figure, being quite sensuous, "I've always thought it was a shame for a single person to take up a whole table. A party of several might come in and not find one."

Well, that was a kindly thought. He supposed that he agreed with her, largely.

She said, looking down at the menu, "I've never eaten here before; is there any particular specialty?"

He made suggestions and she too ordered Hungarian.

His dishes came first and he took them from the automated table center and placed them before him. The wine bottle had already been uncorked and he poured his glass half-full and then savored the bouquet.

She said, "By the way, I suppose we should introduce ourselves. My name's Clara Maritano."

He smiled at her and said, "I'm Kingsley Cusack."

Her eyes widened. "Not *Doctor* Kingsley Cusack?"

"I'm afraid so."

"The author of *The Way of the Mayan?*"

"Why, yes. I'm surprised you knew. The book's been in the library data banks for only a few days. It still hasn't had many reviews—so far as I know."

"Oh, I'm a Mayan buff," she said. "I've already read it. It's wonderful."

"Well, thank you very much," Kingsley said, obviously flattered. "I hope the powers-that-be feel the same. I'm told that it's possibly a bit too controversial."

"Oh, not at all," she told him. "I was particularly fascinated by your description of the House of the Governors in Uxmal and practically everything you said about Chichen Itza."

Kingsley frowned a little at that, even as he started in on his veal with its rich paprika sauce. He had gotten used to chilis down in Mexico and the heat of the dish didn't bother him. The thing was, he hadn't spent much time on Chichen Itza, not thinking it particularly representative of the Mayans. It belonged to an era when the Toltecs had come down from the north and conquered the country. But it was a great tourist center, being greatly reconstructed, and most persons not very well informed on Yucatan usually thought of it first when you mentioned the Mayans.

Her own food had come and now she too set to eating, but still looking into his face as though he was the most interesting thing that had ever happened to her. It was a bit disconcerting.

He said carefully, "What did you think of the chapter on Mayan food?"

"Oh, I was fascinated. I'd give anything to be able to try some of those dishes."

There was no chapter in the book on Mayan food. The book was devoted to the social system and the religion of the Mayans.

Kingsley Cusack didn't consider himself as handsome as all that. He was unaccustomed to having beautiful girls pick him up. Besides that, boyish face or no, he was a bit out of her age group. He rather doubted that her interest in him was romantic and she had just proven that it wasn't intellectual.

In short, what in the hell was this all about? He had been in Yucatan for almost eight years, so it could hardly be something dealing with the period before that. She would have been just a kid eight years ago. No, it had to be something that had evolved since his return. And only one thing of any importance whatsoever had evolved since his return.

She made no more blunders throughout the rest of the meal by avoiding discussing the book and keeping her questions to matters pertaining to present-day Yucatan and the life he had led there. He went along with her. She was a good listener.

When they had finished, they put their dishes back on the table center, and stuck their Universal Credit Cards in the table slot for payment to be deducted.

He said, "How would you like to drop up to the apartment for an after-lunch liqueur? I have quite an extensive library on the Mayans; you might like to look it over."

"I'd love to! Such an opportunity!"

He followed her to the elevator bank and into one of the compartments, noting in passing that she had beautiful buttocks. He said, "You'll have to identify yourself to the elevator's identity screen, before it will let you go up to the residential floors."

"Oh, no," she smiled. "I live in the building, too. My face is registered in the data banks."

Well, that didn't surprise him too much, since she'd been there in the Balkan Room. He had hoped to be able to check if that Clara Maritano name she'd given him was authentic, and also to learn what her identification number was so that he could check back on her. It was one of the reasons he had invited her to his place.

As they approached his apartment the identity screen picked him up and his door opened automatically. He let her precede him inside, and they went into his-living-room-cum-library-and-study.

He said, "Sit down, Clara. How would you like a barack?" He headed for the autobar.

"What's barack?" she said, going over to his desk and, seemingly idly, looking at the stack of notes he had already accumulated next to his vocotyper.

"The Hungarian national spirits. It's based on apricots."

"All right," she agreed.

While he dialed, she said, idly, "What are you working on now? What follows the Mayans?"

"An account of the early Rome at the time of the Tarquin reges."

She said easily, "And are you researching it on the dream machine?"

He came back with the drinks and handed one to her. He sat down and looked at her. "What dream machine?" he said flatly.

She went over to the couch and sat down facing him. She took a small sip of the potent liqueur before saying, still easily, "Let's not fence, Dr. Cusack. You're not stupid. I found that out when I realized that you knew I understood precious little about Mayans. In actuality, I had skim-read your book but largely couldn't make heads or tails of it. No background."

"What dream machine?" he said.

She said, "Academician Bryce Norman has a programmed dream machine in his custody. While on vacation, he's turned it over to you. You're researching your new book on it, King."

He looked at her and said, "Even if I admitted that there was such an unlikely thing, what has it got to do with you, Clara?"

She took another sip of her liqueur and leaned back on the couch and closed her eyes. "Kingsley Cusack," she said, as though reciting. "Doctorate in Ethnology. Thirty-eight years of age. Source of income, Guaranteed Annual Income. Never has held down a job in his life. Like more than ninety percent of the population can do all the work necessary, what with computers and automation. You're not one of the ten percent."

She opened her eyes again. She no longer seemed to be quite as young as he had first thought, and there was even a certain harshness in her voice.

She said, "How does it feel to have no income whatsoever save the government dole, Doctor Cusack?"

"A bit sparse," he said with wry self-deprecation.

"And how would you like to be rich, Doctor Cusack?"

He bowed his head to her. "Believe me, Miss Maritano, all my life I have dreamed of being rich.

80

Among other reasons, it would enable me to fulfill a good many projects I have desired to go into in my field of research but have never been able to afford.''

"Very well,'' she told him. "You now have your chance to get very rich indeed.''

"Indeed?''

"Yes, indeed. I represent a group, Doctor Cusack, that wishes the plans of that dream machine. We are willing to place in a Swiss credit account one million pseudo-dollars, in your name.''

"For just what? I don't have the plans for the thing. I have only the vaguest idea of how it works. You certainly couldn't just carry it out of the building, even if I would let you. The Longfellow Building's Security people would be down on you like a ton of bricks. Besides, the academician is my best friend. I couldn't betray him by peddling his equipment.''

"You wouldn't have to,'' she said, knocking back the balance of the drink. "All we want is for you to let a couple of our technicians into the apartment to study it, uninterrupted for, say, forty-eight hours.''

"And for that you'd pay me a million pseudo-dollars?''

"Yes, King.''

"Why?'' he said. "What in the world do you plan doing with it?''

She smiled, cynically, and said, "Suppose you were a ninety-year-old man, who was also a billionaire. What would you pay, per hour, to use that machine? To project yourself into Mark Antony, barging down the Nile with Cleopatra. What would you pay, per hour, to spend an evening in one of those famous turn-of-the-century bordellos in Paris? What would you pay to divorce yourself from a diet of gruel and fruit juices, and experience the eating of the grandest banquets come down through the ages?''

''I see,'' Kingsley said. ''But admitting such a machine, who would be so low as to seduce it to such an end?''

''Me,'' she said. ''And the group I represent. Who would be harmed? Most very rich men are old men. What harm would be done if they spent part of their final years enjoying themselves, rather than dying inch by inch in discomfort?''

''Where did you learn—or rather think you learned—about this ridiculous-sounding machine?''

''What difference does it make? We learned. And you've already admitted it exists, so there's no use in calling it ridiculous. There are too many people in on the secret, King. One man can keep a secret, possibly two can, but from then on it gets more difficult geometrically. Not even the Manhattan Project was free completely of leaks.''

He finished his own drink and put the glass down on the cocktail table next to his chair.

He said, very slowly, ''Miss Maritano, I guess it's just that I don't need a million pseudo-dollars that badly. But even if I did, I suspect that I would not turn its workings over to your group.''

She sighed and said, ''Think it over, King. But you don't have too long. The technicians would probably need the full forty-eight hours to figure this thing out. The academician was to be gone for only two weeks and part of that time has already elapsed. By the way, the million would be deposited to your account *before* you allowed them into Bryce Norman's escape sanctum, so there would be no chance of bad faith.'' She stood up, preparatory to leaving. "I'll stay in touch.''

He followed her to the door and let her out.

"Adios, Miss Maritano,'' he said.

"Hasta luego.'' She smiled at him mockingly.

He watched after her for a moment as she headed for the elevators. He still thought she had remarkable buttocks, and sighed.

He closed the door behind him and went back to the autobar and dialed himself another barak. He took it back to his chair and sat down again.

She had called him King. There was only one person in the world who called him that: Bryce Norman. She had also mentioned Mark Antony barging down the Nile with Cleopatra. It was an example Bryce had used when telling Kingsley about the workings of the dream programmer.

Kingsley didn't like it. He knocked back the strong spirits and stood again. He went over to his phone screen and dialed the building's security and said, "This is Doctor Cusack, Apartment 1328. Under no circumstances is this door to be opened to anyone save myself, on proper identification by the identity screen, until further notice. Not even building maintenance workers.''

"Yes, Doctor Cusack,'' the security man said.

He left his apartment and took the elevator up to that of the academician.

He immediately went to the phone screen in the living room and dialed security again.

He said, when the other had faded in, "This is

Doctor Kingsley Cusack of Apartment 1328. Academician Bryce Norman has left me in charge of his quarters while away on vacation. He is on a cruise, probably in the Caribbean. You can undoubtedly check through the travel reservations, or call him on his identification on his transceiver, where he is. Get his permission if you need; however, I want this apartment sealed, except for me. No one is to enter it, even building maintenance personnel, without my permission. Even if they have a key. In short, only I am to be able to enter, until his return. This is a matter of national security. Undoubtedly, the academician will explain further upon his return, but meanwhile I repeat, this is a matter of national security and of the greatest importance.''

The security man looked impressed. "Very well, Doctor Cusack. We will check with the academician, but pending reaching him, your orders will be carried out. It will be impossible for anyone to enter the academician's apartment except yourself, or with your permission.'' His face faded from the screen.

Kingsley Cusack now began a tour of the apartment. He was in a field unknown to him. Such information as he had had been picked up by watching old crime and suspense vision-tapes. He looked behind paintings, he carefully searched about the various phone screens, autoteachers and library boosters in the apartment.

Finally he found it behind a painting, in the escape sanctum where he should have known from the first it would be.

A small electronic device. He knew what it was. An electronic bug. Supposedly they didn't exist any more.

The day of the tap was supposedly over. But this existed, all right. And he assumed that any competent electronics technician could construct one. The blueprints would be in the International Data Banks, no matter how antiquated the use of the things.

In short, whatever the group to which Clara Maritano belonged, it had bugged the academician's escape sanctum and had undoubtedly listened in on whatever conversation he'd had with Kingsley Cusack.

They would know about the dream programmer, including how to operate it. They would have all the information that Kingsley had received from his friend.

He broke the damned thing and then decided not to return to his own apartment. He didn't want to be out in the halls, going back and forth.

In the morning, he dithered for quite a time, after breakfast, before deciding to take on another few hours of dream. He had spent the balance of the previous day working on his notes, utilizing the academician's vocotyper. The notes were accumulating rapidly, since each time he entered the mind of Horatius the Roman was older and hence had considerably more accumulated knowledge to tap. The whole thing continued to confuse him. When in the dreams, he *was* Horatius . . . but still he was himself.

Chapter Nine

Rome—Phipe Horatius Cocles

And again, as I hurried down from our home on the Palatine hill to the festival I felt the strangeness enter my mind. By now, I could ignore it, especially in view of the urgency of my mission. My return to Rome from the battle near Tibur and other campaigns coincided with the festival of the Bacchanalia, our fete in honor of the god of wine, Bacchus. It was quite the most drunken orgy of the year and one that didn't ordinarily interest me. But this time was different. I hurried to the Forum and to the Temple of Vulcan.

And there she stood where she must be, costumed again as a nymph and her mask in place. She looked as though she had stood there for some time, peering anxiously at the strange faces in the crowds, and she must have more than once been bothered by reeling drunkards who were everywhere. How could she have known that I would return this day? For know she evidently did, possibly even as I had known that she would still remain unwed.

I slipped up behind her and said, "Fair nymph, do you need the protection of a soldier?"

She turned sharply in irriation and for the briefest of moments did not recognize me, for indeed I now wore a black beard where I had been clean shaven when I had departed on the various campaigns Valerius had led us through.

"No, I do not," she said haughtily. "And I do not wish to be . . . *Phipe*!"

"Carmenta!"

Aye! how does one tell of the meeting of first lovers, reunited after a long separation? Her mask kept her lips from mine, nor would she remove it. But we most hold and gush forth meaningless words, and she must cry a bit, and all of a sudden there was great need for us to be alone.

Hurriedly, we bought a small skin of wine and various food dainties, trying as best we could to recall exactly what we had purchased that first time we had met at the Saturnalia. And we carried it, as before, up the Clivus Capitolinus and to the still-unfinished Temple of the Capitoline Triad, where work was now proceeding in the interior; the building was soon to be ready for consecration. It would have been difficult for me to foresee that this would go so quickly. Where were Carmenta and I to meet when it was completed?

And then we found our own true spot, even as the sun was setting, and wine and food were forgotten as I took my darling in my arms, and she, her own hands trembling, removed her mask. At first I was taken aback, for I had left my Carmenta little more than a child, and now she was a woman full, so much had the few months affected her.

She looked at me wonderingly and reached forth a hand to touch my beard. "Are you truly my Phipe?"

"And you my Carmenta?"

And then we could hold back no longer and her lips were again mine, and her breasts were woman beneath my palms. She whimpered even as she kissed me, and when I held her tighter, held me tighter still. And my Carmenta was all female and quite as incapable of resisting my ardent needs as I was to think of the danger to which I was submitting her innocence.

I had spread my cloak upon the ground for us both to sit, but now she was sprawled upon it and my lips had wandered far afield from her own. Her eyes were closed and her face flushed and she murmured incoherently as I practiced upon her, unthinkingly, some of the love tricks I had learned in the towns where the cohort had tou :hed during the campaign. And, unused to such, or even to as much as a man's kiss during the same period, she was incapable of resisting my advance and soon her murmuring was turned to moaning and finally she seized my head and cried for me to stop. So stop I did and sat up to remove some of my own clothing, for Carmenta was now stretched out before me, her limbs akimbo, and nude to my gaze. Her body was perfect, in youth and virginity, and gleamed cream and white with only the golden pubic hair a break in the texture.

She moved her legs to accommodate me, bending them instinctively, and such the extent of her needs that I had little difficulty in penetrating her, though she gave one sharp cry as her hymen fell to my victorious assault. I rode her in love and so meant was she for the act of love that within moments she had found the correct rhythm and moved with me, reaching up her hips for the benefit of my full thrust each time I drove deep. And though I understand this is most unusual, she successfully reached her climax this first time she ever experienced coitus.

Afterwards, as we lay panting, the cloak now pulled over us since although Rome is not bitter cold in mid-December, it is still far from warm, she moaned, "Oh, Phipe, I should never have . . ."

I told her comfortingly, "Nothing else was possible, my Carmenta. It was as fated as though every haruspex in Italy had foreseen it."

"But I should not——"

"But we had to."

She remained quiet for a moment and then sighed and said, "Yes, but we had to."

And now that the first flowing of passion had ebbed for the time we were able to talk beyond the murmuring of endearments. In a manner, it was a strange conversation, for although I told her freely of all that had transpired with me since last I had seen her, and she was keenly interested in every detail, still she in turn would tell me nothing of her own personal experiences, of her home life or of her people. All she had to relate were city matters or public gossip. For instance, my friend Mamilius, she revealed, had won Tarquina, daughter of Tarquin, and there had been a suitable marriage, the ceremony of which Carmenta had evidently attended; and Mamilius had returned with his bride to Tusculum.

It was expected he might soon be elected to take up the duties of the rex, since his father was aged.

And, another matter, there had been an evil portent in Rome not long before. It seemed as though a snake crawled out of the altar while Tarquin Superbus was sacrificing to his home lars and penates. No augur but must brand this the most disastrous of signs.

I told her of my friend Astur, who since I had seen him last had become *marniu* of far northern Luna, acting in capacity of lucumo of the town, although appointed from Volterra rather than being elected. He was now married to an Etruscan girl named Velia, and both of them corresponded with me. I had written them of Carmenta, and in her last letter Velia had told me that I must elope with my patrician sweetheart and come to live in Luna.

Carmenta was silent for a long moment and then said, her voice low and musing, "No. Even that would not be far enough. They would come for me."

"I was but jesting," I told her. "How could either of us leave Rome?"

She looked at me strangely. "But you have left Rome before and sometimes for years on end. Why is it so unthinkable that we leave together, never to return?"

"Why . . ." I scowled, not at her but at the idea. "Why, we're Romans. Nowhere else would we really be happy."

"But weren't you happy when you attended school in Caere? When you described it and your close friends and relatives there, you sounded as though you were."

I said, disturbed, "In a way, perhaps. But that was

temporary, and it was necessary for my studies. But we are Romans and Rome is our city. You would probably dislike the Etruscans, finding their ways different. Even I sometimes find it difficult to acclimate myself to being among them, and, as you say, I have spent years in Eturia.''

Carmenta sighed and in the dim light of night her face seemed ethereally childlike as of yore. ''I suppose so,'' she said. ''Everyone knows that Rome is the greatest city in the world, and the best in which to reside.'' But she turned her head aside and stared up at the columns of the temple which reared above us.

That was not quite what I had meant. Indeed, any Etruscan town of size was more comfortable than Rome, the streets paved, the sewer system perfected, the public buildings beautiful and more profuse than in our own city. It was not these things. It was just that we were *Romans* and no other city would do for us. I felt oddly impatient, but whether it was with her, or with myself, I could not say.

We dallied some more, though we did not repeat the ultimate experience of which man and woman are capable, and the hours passed too quickly and then she must return to her home.

The Bacchanalia had only begun and she felt quite certain that she could return again the next day, and so we planned it.

''However,'' I said, frowning. ''There is some possibility that I will be sent on a mission for Tarquin, the rex. My father is now quite aged and is no longer available for his missions to the Etruscans. Since I speak the language and am familiar with their institutions, perhaps his mantle will fall upon my shoulders. If he has some such order for me that will prevent my meeting you tomorrow night, shall I send a messenger to you?"

"No. Oh, no," she said hurriedly. "I don't wish to talk to anyone but you. If you cannot come, I will understand and simply return each evening as long as the Bacclanalia continues. And after that, such nights as I can get away from . . . home."

As ever before, I was allowed to escort her no further than to the Vulcanal. When she was gone from view I turned on my heel and made my way to our home on the Palatine.

If I thought that Carmenta had changed so greatly during my absence in Luna, then the appearance of my father shocked me. For in that short period his hair had gone largely white, while before there had been but a tint of gray at his temples. I realized that Celer was growing old and that this was the reason Tarquin seemed to be considering breaking me into the role my father had held so long. It has been said that as a man ages, his basic character shows increasingly in his face, so that if a man be a miser, his stinginess and love of money is there to be read, or if he is overly sensuous, his face becomes gross. And my father's face? In his age, it had become increasingly stern, resolute, perhaps indominable, and I could read there no love for ought other than his duty to Rome. And I felt sadness in me to see this, for I loved my father and knew his great sorrow when my mother, Larthia, had died. He had never remarried.

I told him of my experiences and my opinions on the

fighting abilities of the various peoples Valerius had led us against, including the Etruscan raiders. I came to the opinion that Celer Horatius would probably report to his political friends that which would interest them. I asked him how such matters were developing and he seemed of the belief that things were coming so quickly to a head that there must be drastic changes made in Rome in the very near future.

I said, "Then perhaps the Sibyl was correct, that Tarquin is so hated that he will be driven from his office and be Rome's last rex."

Father shook his head and grimaced as though disliking the manner in which I had put it. "You must realize, my son, that in such matters the individual makes little difference. Some there are, such as Brutus, who literally hate Tarquin Superbus, for personal reasons. Such men are not the type to direct the destinies of Rome which should be in the hands of men motivated by higher ideals than personal ones. I can assure you that I don't hate Tarquin Superbus. In fact, I think him one of the most capable reges our city has had."

I admit to having been surprised. "But you actively work to overthrow him."

"I work to overthrow the office he holds, the institution of rex, not any individual man. I would so work, no matter who held the office, were it the god Mars himself. You see, my son, the institution is outworn and must be destroyed. It no longer fits the conditions that apply in Rome, and if we are to maintain our Roman liberties and be allowed to pursue our individual fortunes as best our abilities provide for, then such institutions as the rex and government based on a senate appointed from the gentes must go.''

In the past I had assimilated bits and pieces of my father's political philosophy, but this was the first time I could recall that he had put it into a whole.

I said, ''But why, if the office of rex was once part of a democratic society, should be change? Surely, it is just a matter of putting a good man in the position, or perhaps some minor reforms.''

''No, Phipe.'' He was shaking his head dourly. ''In the days of Romulus and Numa Pompilius, our society was a simple one. The Senate, composed of a representative from each gens in the city, and an Assembly of the People, could easily handle our governing. A popularly elected rex could handle both military affairs and act as chief priest. But that was long ago and Rome was a simple agricultural center, problems few, and population small. Now, however, so many complications have been added that the old institutions cannot take care of them. New officials have to be found to handle newly arisen problems. Take just one. In the days of Romulus there was no such thing as money and all trade was handled by barter. But now Rome grows rich, through trade and war, and we have gold coins from Sicily and silver ones from Carthage and Greece, though largely we use the bronze Etruscan *ase rude* for our medium of exchange. But soon we must mint our own Roman coinage and that will involve various offices pertaining to a treasury.''

I said, ''But how does this involve the rex?''

''In the past, Phipe, the rex was both head of the army and pontus maximus, two important positions but not overly involved. To be head of the army, Romulus simply got out in front of the spearmen, waved his sword in the direction of the enemy, shouted the charge and led them to victory. Religion, too, was simple, temples nonexistent, in backward Rome, so his priesthood involved little more than occasionally sacrificing an animal to the gods. But now we have two or three armies in the field at any given time and, as new temples to new gods go up all about town, we have colleges of priests that number into the hundreds.

"Far from personally being able to handle the responsibilities which are his duty, he must delegate practically everything, and hence has built up a large staff of clerks, secretaries, assistants, and toadies. And as the problems of financing our wars today become ever greater his tendency is to try and control such matters as taxes, customs, tribute from the conquered cities, and such sources of finance. When new offices must be initiated, he attempts to dominate them, bringing what pressures he can to have his followers named. Police were unknown when Rome began to grow on these seven hills, but our lives have become so complicated that now we need their protection. Who controls the police? The rex, who has announced that they are in truth a portion of the army, which comes under his jurisdiction."

I said, thinking it out slowly, "Perhaps it is best to have such a strong man at the head of the state."

He shook his head definitely. "No. Give up your democratic liberties at your peril, my son. True, it sometimes seems that a certain individual governs benevolently, but once you have the institution of tyranny, how can you be guaranteed that your next tyrant and the next will be equally benevolent? No, if Rome is to fulfill her destiny, it will be through the workings of free men, and since the office of rex is no longer compatible with freedom, it must go. I bear no malice toward Tarquin, but so long as he continues to hold the office of rex, then I am his opponent.''

Chapter Ten

Princeton—Kingsley Cusack

This time when Kingsley awakened from the dream he realized that he had flubbed it again. He had spent most of the dream he had programmed for him with Horatius and his girl friend in the same remote spot on the Capitol hill that they had gone to the first time they had met. Of course, he had seen some of the Bacchanalia, but it wasn't greatly different from the Saturnalia—a great many drunks and sex-inflamed celebrants. And he'd had the experience of coming down all the way from the Palatine hill and walking through the Forum to where Horatius had met Carmenta, and later returning and seeing a typical Roman household. In the opinion of Kingsley Cusack, the Forum wasn't as all that impressive in the days of the Tarquin kings. He supposed that it didn't reach its full glory until the days of Augustus and the other Julian emperors, who had turned it into a city of marble where once it had been brick. In Horatius' day Rome was no more than a city-state, and far from the most prominent on the Italian peninsula.

However, though his latest dream had not given him much in the way of new material, he had acquired memories from the mind of Horatius. He sat himself down at the vocotyper to make notes.

He had a good many notes he wanted to make, particularly dealing with the conspiracy against Tarquin which was developing and with the campaigns Horatius had been through with Valerius; but then the phone screen buzzed.

Impatiently, he flicked off the vocotyper and activated the phone.

Bryce Norman's face was there, obviously worried. The academician said, "King, the security people of the Longfellow Building have gotten in touch with me, here on the ship. They said that you gave them rather strange orders, preventing even building maintenance workers from entering my apartment. I okayed your orders, of course, but is there anything special up?"

Kingsley said unhappily, "Bryce, the first day you were gone two men came to the door. I doubt if they were connected with the university. I got the impression that they had a key and were about to enter the apartment when I opened the door——"

"Nobody has a key except you, and me of course, and the building authorities."

Kingsley said, "For all I know they might have had some special key that would open the door. Those things that burglars have in the old crime movies, skeleton keys or whatever they called them. They wanted to know how long you'd be gone, and wanted to come in and look around."

"What did you do," the academician asked.

"Sent them packing. One of them said something about going to report to the boss."

"What boss?"

"I don't know. That's all I know."

"That doesn't seem to be enough to get into such a tissy about. Perhaps it was a couple of men who had some business with me."

Kingsley said, "They seemed to know that you were gone, Bryce. At least I got that impression. And they were surprised to see me. But the thing is, that's not all. Yesterday I was approached by a girl. She offered me a million pseudo-dollars for the opportunity to have some technicians examine the machine."

"You mean that you told her about it! I specifically warned you——"

Kingsley shook his head. "No. She already knew. Someone had planted an electronic bug here in your escape sanctum. Later, I managed to find it and destroy it. However, they had obviously listened to all the conversations we had between ourselves."

"My God! This is supposed to be the most highly guarded secret in the country. Do you know how many of those machines are in existence?"

"You gave me the opinion very few."

"Exactly one. It's an experimental model. We're testing it all ways from Tuesday before going on with the experiment. I told you of the two associates who fouled up on it, one of them to the point of going nearly mad. It was probably one of them who leaked the information. At any rate, we're treading just as slowly and carefully as we can. We realize what potential dynamite it is. Kingsley, guard that machine with your life. I'm at sea now and I think it will be a couple of days, at least, before we land at some port with facilities for my flying back. Some of these islands are still quite remote."

"Okay," Kingsley said. "I consider myself under siege. Shouldn't you let me get in touch with someone else in your group? Warn them?"

The academician thought about it before saying, "No, confound it all. If you made such a report, first they would know I broke my word in telling you about it and probably would suspect that I allowed you its use. Second, they would undoubtedly take it away from me, to continue the experiment in some other spot, and with some more reliable investigator than I have proven to be. No, sit tight. The fat's in the fire, but I'll be back as soon as possible."

The face faded. Kingsley flicked the screen off and looked at it for a long moment.

"Holy smokes," he said. "Only one in the whole world and I'm sitting on it. I'd gotten the impression that there were at least a couple of hundred of them."

He was still mulling it over when the identity screen on the door buzzed. He looked up impatiently, came to his feet, left the escape sanctum, and crossed the living room to the door. He activated the screen.

It was one of the goons.

Kingsley could see him and the indistinct face of his companion behind him, but he knew the others couldn't see him. The screen was one-way.

Aggravated, and still upset enough not to be thinking clearly, he made the mistake of snatching open the door and snarling, "What the hell do you want? The academician isn't here. Perhaps he'll be back in two or three days. Now go on away.''

The first one put out his heavy hand, flat, and pushed Kingsley Cusack backward, following him quickly. He pushed again.

The second one came into the apartment as well, closing the door behind him. The faces of both men were expressionless. Even under these circumstances, the thought came into Kingsley's mind these two watched old time crime films for their entertainment and were trying to look like Capone men.

The first one said, ''My name's Joe and this here is Rocky. We're very friendly guys. Sit.'' He pushed Kingsley down into an easy chair and said to his companion, ''Case the joint, Rocky.''

Kingsley, through his astonishment, blurted, ''Why, you sonofabitch, you can't do this. You've illegally entered this apartment.''

''My heart is pumping piss,'' Joe said.

Kingsley began to struggle to his feet but Joe pushed him down again and said, ''Look, friend, I've got fifty pounds on you. And besides that, guess what? Both me and Rocky is expugs. Prize fighters, see? I bet you never been in a fist fight in your life. You're the professor type, even if you can't get no job at your trade. So, why don't you take it easy?''

Kingsley Cusack was so enraged that he sputtered.

Rocky came back into the room. ''It's in there, all right,'' he said, gesturing toward the escape sanctum with his head.

Joe nodded and said to Kingsley, ''Okay, chum-pal, on your feet. We're going to see the boss.''

"The hell we are," Kingsley snapped. "You're not getting me out of here, and, what's more, the first opportunity I have I'm going to bring security down on you like a ton of bricks."

Rocky grinned at him and brought a largish knife from his pocket. He touched a stud on its side and a vicious-looking blade flicked out. Rocky made wide circling motions with it, in the manner of a knife fighter.

He said, "You'd be surprised how quick I am with this, chum-pal. You'd be surprised how quick I can get it out and into a guy's guts. Or, if he's running, how well I can throw it and how far. Now, we're getting out of here. So come along, the boss wants to talk to you, is all. Just talk. He's got some sort of proposition."

Kingsley Cusack, although furious, was no fool. These men were thugs, though this was an age in which you didn't expect to run into such. What their orders were, if he didn't comply, he didn't know; but he suspected they were not above even more violence than they had so far exerted. He stood, in resignation.

One of them walked ahead of him, one followed. They left the apartment, carefully closing the door behind them.

From time to time, as they made their way to the car pool in the basement, they passed others. Kingsley considered the possibility of shouting for help and making a run for it, but rejected the idea. People in this era simply were not used to violence and he doubted that anyone would come to his assistance within a reasonable length of time. And he also suspected that the one called Rocky had not been exaggerating when he had described his efficiency with his blade. At least, they didn't seem to have guns. But, of course, guns were unknown these days. At long last the authorities had really suppressed them. Even those in the museums usually had the firing pin, or some other vital part of the mechanism, removed.

They took an elevator to the car pool in the basement and Joe calmly summoned an electrosteamer hover-car. He got into the front with Kingsley, and Rocky got into the back, immediately behind their captive. Through all this they were very cheerful when they addressed him.

They emerged from the Longfellow Building and immediately dipped down into the first outlet of the automated underground ultrahighways.

Rocky said with mock apology, "And this, chum-pal, is where we give you a little shot that'll dim your peepers a bit."

"Oh, no you don't," Kingsley said in alarm and tried to spin.

But he was too late. He could feel the prick of the needle in his shoulder.

Chapter Eleven

Location Unknown—Kingsley Cusack

Kingsley Cusack had not even known that there was such a drug and when it first became effective he was terrified. His vision dimmed, and then departed completely. He was blind.

"You blinded me, you bastard!" he yelled.

Rocky was soothing. "It's only temporary, Doc," he said. "It wears off in no time atall. Besides, it's more comfortable than a blindfold." He chuckled. "And not so damned conspicuous."

They drove for a while in silence, seemingly under automated control, and then left the underground highway and eventually entered a building.

Very solicitously they took him by the arms and led him. On the face of it, any observers would think that Kingsley Cusack was a blind man. They walked him a way and then entered an elevator. It zipped them upward. Kingsley realized that this must be a high-rise building with as many floors, possibly, as the Longfellow Building. He was attempting to retain all the details that he could; everything he could about these two men, everything about the drive they had taken him on, its duration and so forth. The fact that they had summoned a car would mean that there would be a record of the transaction in the data banks. They said that their names were Joe and Rocky and that both were expugilists, a type of sportsman that wasn't very common these days. Of course, all that, including their names, could be lies.

The elevator came to a halt and they emerged, the two thugs still holding his arms. They proceeded down a hall. There were no impressions he could get here that would help. The elevator ride had lasted quite a time so they must be in the higher reaches of the building.

They stopped before what he supposed was a door and Joe said, "Joe."

They entered an apartment and advanced quite a distance before coming to a halt.

Rocky said, "Here he is, Boss. We've got him on dimout, so he can't see."

"Give him back his vision," a calm, authoritive voice said.

Kingsley felt another needle prick. One of his two captors pushed him down into a chair. Within minutes, his vision began to clear. It had been one of the damnedest experiences of his life. Blindness is a terrifying condition.

His surroundings began to fade in, at first dimly; he realized that he was in a very large escape sanctum. At first he didn't realize it when his vision was back to normal, since, for some reason, the room was very poorly lighted. Drapes were drawn at the window so that he had no way of placing the location of the building they had brought him to.

Behind the large wooden desk, an antique, sat a man wearing a business suit, who, of all things, had a black mask over his face, a large black mask covering all of his features. He had a strong build, and the two hands which he had flat on the desk before him were chubby and white; the hands of a man who didn't work and who saw too little of the sun.

Kingsley Cusack looked about the room. It was furnished and decorated in such fashion that it was obvious that the owner had no need to worry about expense. And the interior decorator was obviously a top man in his field.

But it was more than just an escape sanctum, albeit the largest Kingsley had ever seen; it was also in the way of being a museum. A museum of older weapons. There was even a complete suit of armor standing in one corner, and a crossbow, with a quiver of quarrels, on one of the walls. But the collection was mostly of swords and daggers, the weapons of the Middle Ages and before.

The man behind the desk said, ''I see that you appreciate my humble collection, which is understandable in view of your history and anthropology interests.'' The voice was an educated and cultivated one.

Rocky was leaning idly against the door. Joe had reversed a chair and was sitting on it astraddle, near one of the bookcases.

Kingsley said tightly, ''I don't give a damn about your collection of overgrown knives. I've been kidnapped. The apartment which had been left in my charge was invaded against my will and, with my life threatened, I was forced to come here. You have a lot to answer for.''

"Not at all, Doctor Cusack," the other said soothingly. "My instructions to my men were to invite you to visit me. I am afraid that they became overenthusiastic. I have a business proposition to make to you.''

"Nonsense," Kingsley snapped. "If this is merely a business matter, I could just get up and walk out. Is that all right with you? And why in the hell are you so cloak and dagger as to be wearing a mask? What are you trying to hide?''

The other ignored the second part of the question and said, still evenly, "You will be perfectly free to leave shortly, Doctor Cusack. My men will return you to the Longfellow Building and to either your own apartment or to that of Academician Norman. I note, by the way, that you have evidently located and destroyed the electronic bug in the good academician's escape room.''

That set Kingsley back somewhat. He had assumed that it was Carla Maritano's group who had bugged the apartment. How else could she have known so much about the dream programmer?

But he could think about that development later. He said, making no attempt to keep the irritation out of his voice, "All right, what's this big proposition? I want to get out of here.''

"Ummm. Very well, let us say, Doctor Cusack, that I represent interests that have thought out some of the ramifications of the dream programmer that even Academician Norman has not stumbled upon. As a result, we are willing to pay a most generous sum for the device.''

"It's not for sale."

The other ignored him. "We are willing to pay two million pseudo-dollars, Kingsley Cusack. Tax free and deposited any place you wish."

Kingsley said impatiently, "Look, even if I wanted to make such a deal with you, you could never get it out of the place without drawing all sorts of attention. It's big and it's heavy and I rather suspect that the academician has made some sort of arrangements with security to protect it. Possibly the moment it was unplugged from the International Data Banks and the Intuitive Computer to be moved some sort of signal would be flashed to security of the Longfellow Building, and they'd be on you."

The other picked up a water carafe and began to pour himself a glass, but then cut the motion short, probably realizing that he'd have to lift his mask to drink it.

He said, "We have no need to unplug the machine, Doctor Cusack. We will bring in some technicians to examine it, and to get a sample of the drug which is injected into the dreamer for analysis. We rather doubt that the dream programmer is as complicated as all that. It is largely dependent upon the data banks and the Intuitive Computer and their use is open to all. The academician's group has no monopoly on their use."

Kingsley said cynically, "What do you want it for, to peddle its use to senile old men who want one last fling before kicking off?"

"Certainly not," the other said in contempt. "My colleagues and I are above such mundane usage of the greatest invention the world has ever seen."

"Well," Kingsley said, "if you're so open and

aboveboard, why not just approach Bryce Norman and state your case? Possibly this group can amalgamate with yours and you can both use it.''

Joe laughed softly.

The man behind the desk said, without raising his voice, ''That will be all, Joe.''

The man behind the desk said, ''I am afraid that is out of the question. I doubt if our need of the dream programmer would meet with the approval of the altruistic academician and his associates.''

Kingsley was curious now. And also he wanted to get as much more information as possible from this character, so that he could turn it over to Bryce Norman on his return.

He said, ''What's this ramification that the academician hasn't stumbled upon? What is it that you want the machine for?''

The other obviously didn't like that. He said slowly, ''I . . . I don't think I can tell you that, Doctor Cusack.''

''Then you sure as hell aren't going to get into that apartment to check it out. I've already informed security that no one is to get in without my permission.''

And the other obviously didn't like that either. He remained silent for a moment. Finally he sighed and said, ''Let us put it this way, Doctor. I represent certain political elements in the United States of the Americas. The dream programmer would be priceless to us.''

Kingsley didn't get it. He said, ''Politics? What possible use could it be in politics?''

The other man nodded and said, ''As I say, it would be priceless, Doctor Cusack. You and your academician friend are using it to research history of the far past. But suppose we utilized it to, ah, *research* more recent history? Suppose we had a political figure who stood in our way. Perhaps a senator, perhaps even a president. Using the dream machine, we could go back a few years in our opponent's career and find out his innermost secrets. No man, especially a politician, but has his secret life which he does not wish to be revealed. It might be that he is having a love affair; it might be that he is secretly a homosexual; it might be embezzlement or income tax fraud; perhaps he has peddled his influence, or lined the nests of his close friends. Yes, every man has his secrets hiding somewhere in his past. The dream programmer would reveal them to us."

Kingsley Cusack was staring at the other man in fascination. He said, "You'd use the equipment for a purpose like that? I have no doubt but that it would work, given the Intuitive Computer. The Big Brother to end all Big Brothers. What would the finality be?"

The other said comfortably, "With it, Doctor, we could overnight wipe the opposition from our path. We offer you two million pseudo-dollars." He added sneeringly "No small amount for an unemployed anthropologist who lives on the governmental Guaranteed Annual Income."

Kingsley suddenly realized that though the man had promised to have him returned to his apartment, he necessarily do so. They might simply dispose of him and take other measures to get into the academician's place. If they had penetrated it sufficiently to conceal that bug, perhaps they could do it again, in spite of the instructions he had given security.

He played it carefully, saying, as though thinking it over, "Your point is well taken. Guaranteed Annual Income is sufficient for moderately comfortable living; however, it keeps you from enjoying all but the necessities of life."

The other nodded approvingly. "I should think it would."

Kingsley said slowly, not wanting to alert his captor by what would seem too easy acceptance, "But the thing is, Bryce Norman is my closest friend, and he trusts me."

The other's voice dripped with reasonableness. "But this would not concern the good academician. He utilizes the device for historical research. We would use it only for political purposes. In fact, if anything, Norman would ultimately profit by our having it, since we would throw the present scoundrels—who enjoy the highest positions in our great land—out and establish a more efficient, more honest administration."

"And I'm an incredibly great lover, rivaling Casanova and Don Juan rolled into one," Kingsley thought inwardly. But he said, aloud, "Well, it's a point. I don't know if I buy it or not."

He stood up and added, "I'll tell you what I'll do. Give me twenty-four hours. I'll let you know at the end of that time. I'm inclined to think I'll take you up." He smiled in self-deprecation. "God knows, I could use two million pseduo-dollars for no more effort than allowing somebody into an apartment for a few hours."

The man behind the desk hesitated for at least a full minute. He obviously had a suspicious mind. He was peering through the holes in his mask at his reluctant visitor's face, obviously, once again, wondering just how reluctant the visitor was.

Finally, he said, "Taken. It's a deal, a bargain then. Joe, Rocky, return Doctor Cusack to his quarters."

Joe got up from his chair and approached. He said, "Sorry, Doc, we got to give you that shot again."

"All right," Kingsley said, extending his arm.

They retraced their route through the building and to its car pool, but once they were out in the open again, in the hover-car, Kingsley got the damnedest feeling that they weren't returning by the same route to the university city. On top of that, he got a very strong feeling that the return didn't take nearly as long as the trip out. What in the world was that adding up to, if anything?

They didn't actually return him to his apartment, but gave him the second shot, the antidote, in the car pool of the Longfellow Building, waited until he had recovered his sight, then let him out of the car and quickly took off.

He supposed that he could have shouted for security, but he suspected that Joe and Rocky would be clear before he could begin to get the alarm over. They were obviously pros in this sort of thing. Instead, he turned and headed for the elevators.

Back in the academician's apartment, he barred the door with its chain and went immediately to the living room's phone screen.

He called the security offices and said to the clean-faced young sergeant who responded, "I'm Doctor

Kingsley Cusack of Apartment one three two four but presently occupying Academician Bryce Norman's apartment until his return from vacation. Yesterday, I requested that no one be allowed to enter this apartment save the academician, of course, and myself. Your office checked with him and he verified my order. However, today two men forced entrance and then compelled me to accompany them on a mission in which I was not interested. Now then, I want a complete check on the identity screen of this apartment. Anyone who stands before it should be photographed. I do not know how those two entered this building. They are neither students nor faculty. If they show up, once more, and I have reason to believe that they will in about twenty-four hours, I'll notify you immediately so that you can apprehend them. This is a matter of national security, sergeant."

The sergeant said something into his vocotyper, and then said to Kingsley, "Yes, Doctor. The academician so informed us. Your instructions will be carried out. Men will be staked out on your floor on a twenty-four-hour-a-day basis."

"Good." Kingsley flicked the phone off.

He ate and returned to his notes. Damn it. Time was running out on him. He wasn't going to get his full two weeks, and he had hardly scratched the surface of the Rome of Horatius' time.

He went to bed earlier than he had planned and decided to take the full eight hours sleep that he usually took, rather than only five hours. He was letting all this pile up; the psychological effects of his experiences with Horatius, plus the attempts on the part of the two

113

different groups to get possession of the dream programmer.

In the morning, he thought carefully before instructing the device. He didn't want to wind up again in Carmenta's loving arms, no matter how pleasant the memory was. He wanted to spend his full eight hours doing something packed full of interesting and instructive material on the Romans and Etruscans.

In his last dream, Horatius had mentioned that possibly Tarquin Superbus, the rex of Rome, might send him into Etruria as an ambassador, or military attaché. That sounded promising to Kingsley Cusack. However, once again he didn't get exactly what he had expected.

Chapter Twelve

The Etruscan City of Volsini—Horatius

It was in the city of Volsini that the probing of the alien mind came for the fifth time. And once again it seemed to be searching my recent memories, besides experiencing my current actions. I put up with it as always, though mystified. What else was there to do?

I had been assigned by Tarquin to accompany his two sons, Lucius and Aruns, on a tour of the twelve cities of the Etruscan Confederation. It was a goodwill tour but also one on which they were to familiarize themselves with the allies, since one day one or the other of them might be elected rex.

"And my duties, sir?" I had asked in my interview with Tarquin in the Regia.

And he had said, "Your role is that of an assistant, a military attaché. However, it will also be your duty to assimilate such military information as is possible. The system of construction and the strength of the walls; the number of men fit to bear arms in each city you visit; the machines of war available; the extent to which military engineering seems to be utilized. You realize, of course, that the state of military competence differs largely between the cities in the league. I wish to know details of this. Such information as this is always valuable. One never knows when our relationship with any of these cities might change for the worse."

My heart had sunk. So I was to be utilized as a common spy. We were not to leave for several days after my interview with Tarquin and I was able to meet Carmenta on two more occasions. Such brief moments, a few hours at a time, in our nook on the Capitoline hill, overlooking all Rome. Such pathetically brief hours. But this time, I assured her, my being away would not be for so long a period and while I was gone I would surely come up with some answer to our problem, for now that she was truly mine and all mine, that answer must be found.

She clung to me and cried, and I could not reassure her. She wailed, "You do not understand. You are all I have. You are my love and my only love." And much more of the same. And our parting was agony.

Our party had rode forth bravely, well mounted, well uniformed, well equipped as befitting Romans embarked upon a state visit to the twelve great cities of the Etruscan Confederation. Lucius and Aruns Tarquin, the sons of the rex, rode ahead, on two white horses; and the rest of us, some twenty in all, followed on blacks. And although both of these offspring of Tarquin had studied in Caere in their time, neither of them were so well acquainted with the old language as I, nor were they so well met with the great families of Etruria though they themselves theoretically belonged to the greatest of all. In reality, the Tarquins had now resided in Rome for over a century and their ways had become Roman ways, so that they counted their descent in the male line, rather than female, and it is doubtful if the Etruscans really considered Lucius and Aruns to be Tarquins at all. So, since I had spent a great deal of my life in Etruria, they brought me into their inner circle and I was a companion rather than simply a military attaché assigned to their staff.

We stopped first at Veii which is but twelve miles from Rome and which we three, at least, had already visited on various occasions. But since this was a state visit to all the important Etruscan cities, Veii too must be included. In fact, she was doubly important on a good will mission since from the founding of Rome there had been bad blood between the two towns.

We stayed in Veii for two weeks and the hospitality, though possibly hypocritical at bottom, was flawless. By day our hosts led us on hunts, or in other pleasurable sport, and by night it was a continual banquet complete with typical Etruscan entertainment. Feminine companionship, as usual, was available and of the highest order; but although Lucius and Aruns responded like the virile men they were, I could not keep my mind from Carmenta and found the idea of bedding another woman repulsive.

Between banquets and other entertainment, I performed my tasks for the rex as best I could, noting the details of fortification, where machine and such advanced equipment as catapults and ballistas were stationed, and similar information. Indeed my heart sank at the prospect of there ever being a war between Rome and Veii for the city is built on a triangular plateau some four hundred feet high and bounded by two streams. At the confluence the sides are quite precipitous, and the strength of the position is doubled at the citadel which is on a promontory above it. The city can be entered only from the northwest angle, and the walls have a circumference of seven miles. To attempt to storm such a fortress was a task, I was convinced, far beyond Rome's present strength and I looked forward to so reporting to Tarquin since the proverbial openheartedness of its inhabitants was honest, and they treated us like gods rather than men during our stay.

Our next stop was Sutri, which we Romans more often call Sutrium, and again I found the city all but impregnable. For good reason is Sutri known as the Gate to Etruria, for no invader from the south could penetrate further into the lands of the confederacy until they had stormed it.

And once again we were met with the openhanded hospitality so prevalent in Etruscan cities and, I must admit, so lacking in Rome. It was as though they would give their all to a friendly stranger, and the Romans of our party were taken aback. In fact, they were somewhat contemptuous, deluding themselves into thinking that their hosts were overdoing matters in the hopes of winning the friendship of Rome. They couldn't have been more wrong.

We stayed two weeks in Sutri, and then passed on to Norchia, Tuscania, Blera, Viterbo, and finally Volsini. Everywhere it was the same, a fine reception given the sons of the rex of Rome, Etruria's ally to the south. In fact, so great was the similarity in the feasting, the sport, the drinking, the hunts, that had it not been for my notes, one city would have blurred into another. But I had particularly looked forward to Volsini, which we Romans call Volsinium, since it was here that my old school friend, Aruns, had recently been elected lucumo.

But there was a sadness in our meeting and one that at first I failed to understand. Aye! we went through the motions, and spent much time speaking of Astur and Mamilius and of Sextus and others we had mutually known in Caere; but something was not there, and finally I knew what it must be. Aruns was lucumo of the city, in charge of its military might and its defense, and he knew me for what I was. For although I came smiling my friendship, I was a spy seeking out information that might one day be used against him, his men, and his city. And he knew it, and I realized that probably everywhere we went the local military heads were aware that I was more than a simple military attaché.

Bitterly my father's image came to my mind. He who had taught me that the greatest thing a man could do was serve Rome. Serve Rome no matter the personal loss, for the Rome dream was such a mighty dream that all else must bow before it.

We remained in the city of Aruns for better than three weeks, and by this time we had been away for four months. And although Aruns was ever correct and as hospitable a host as could be demanded, and although the Volsini folk were as free and as open as those we had met everywhere before, I was ashamed to be present.

And it was here that the alien mind entered my own

and was already scanning my memories and actions when a messenger from Rome overtook our party and delivered dispatches to the two sons of Tarquin. Shortly, they sent for me and when I presented myself, Lucius said, "Your father, Celer, is desperately ill and has asked for you. You have our release from your duties. I would suggest you choose two of the better horses."

I left the tent, my mind in shock. My father was not a young man, but surely he was not so old as to expect serious illness. Not sickness to the death. He was so straight, took such excellent care. He . . . why, nothing could happen to Celer Horatius. Other than Carmenta, I had no one else in all Rome whom I truly loved.

I was packing my few things, my mind still unable to accept the fact that Celer could be seriously ill, when Aruns Tarquin entered the room. He was scowling unhappily in an attempt at sympathy. "I'm sorry to hear of your father, Horatius. He is the best of citizens." He added sourly, "Though not of our party."

I muttered something in the way of thanks and he sank into a chair. "Everything seems to go to the bad at once," he growled restlessly. "Surely there has never been a year with so many bad portents."

I said disinterestedly, even as I continued my hurried preparations, "What has happened now?"

"The worst thing that could happen to the luck of Rome, the gods confound it all. The populous will take it as a strong omen against us Tarquins."

I was thinking of Celer, rather than following the

words of Aruns Tarquin, but I said, automatically, "What is it?"

"They have found one of the Vestals to be with child."

And the cold went through me.

It all dropped upon my shoulders at once, and I could scarce bear the weight, and it was unnecessary to ask the next question; but I heard the words come from my mouth unbidden. "A Vestal? Which one?"

But I knew, *I knew*. And all was clear to me. So clear that I could damn myself for a fool for lack of perception. Her insisting upon mask or hood whilst in public so that none could see her countence . . . Her remaining unwed, in spite of her beauty of face and figure . . . Her freedom of action, so that she was able to meet me at her pleasure, rather than being confined to her father's household . . . Her fear of my learning her identity . . . Her refusal to communicate with me by letter . . . Aye! now all was clear.

Aruns Tarquin was saying bitterly, "The little bitch. She belonged to the Megellus family of the Carmentian gens. I know them well and anybody could have told that she was never meant to be a Vestal Virgin. At the age of twelve she had a figure that could have guaranteed what was to come."

I got out, without turning, keeping my back to him so that he could not see my face, "I don't believe I have ever seen her, but then I've been out of the city so much I seldom attend religious occasions."

"You wouldn't have seen her anyway," he said impatiently. "She was a candidate, taking her novice training. They train for ten years, then for another ten years they perform the Vestal duties, and then for the final ten years they teach the novices. After that, thirty years in all, they retire and are free to marry. Well, our Carmenta couldn't even get through the first ten years."

I said, hard put to keep my voice from sinking into a whisper, "What will they do to her?"

"Didn't you know? Horatius, your religious training has been neglected. She is stripped of her emblems of office, symbolically scourged by my father, the rex, and then buried alive in the Campus Sceleratus."

"And her lover? Have they caught him?"

I knew Aruns Tarquin must have been scowling from his tone of voice, though I could not see him, still not trusting myself to face him and let him see my expression.

He said, "No. She will not reveal his name, evidently."

"Haven't they put her to the question?"

There was shock in his voice. "You can't torture a Vestal Virgin. Only the Pontus Maximus can touch one at all, and only then under strict conditions."

I admittedly wasn't up on such matters. "What if she reveals his name? What happens to the lover?"

He said, as though tiring of the subject, "They flog him to death, the bastard. Can you imagine the luck of all Rome betrayed simply for a woman's tail?"

I pretended to be indignant. I said, "As soon as I have seen to my father, I intend to apply to be captain of her guard until the time comes for her flogging and burial. I shall apply to your father, the rex, himself."

He stared at me in dismay. "You won't have any difficulty in getting the job. It would be the worst of luck to have anything at all to do with the punishment of a Vestal. No one else will want the position."

I wanted it! Somehow or other, I must keep her from talking, from revealing all to Tarquin and the city fathers. If she talked, then all was lost!

Chapter Thirteen

Princeton—Kingsley Cusack

He was getting more used to his awakening after a programmed dream. There was not quite the psychological aftereffects that he had first suffered. But, for that matter, there hadn't been quite as much to experience.

He disengaged himself from the electrodes and left the box and, as usual, sat in the academician's swivel chair at the desk to gather his thoughts.

He had spent most of the eight hours of the dream riding at breakneck speed from Volsini south, so that by the time he reached Sutri both horses were on the verge of collapse, though he had twice switched back and forth. He traded the mounts for two fresh ones and continued the ride, taking time only to snatch at food and wine. It was there that the dream ended. All during the ride, there had been practically nothing in the mind of Horatius, save his father's health and, more pressing still, the need to get to Rome and volunteer to be Carmenta's guard, so that he could prevent her from talking and revealing that he had been her seducer.

Well, at least he had acquired more of the accumulated memories of Horatius which included a wealth of material about several of the major Etruscan cities he had visited with the Tarquin embassy.

He got up and went on into the dining room and ordered his meal, impatient to get to his notes.

The food finished, he returned to the sanctum and sat before the vocotyper. He particularly wanted to record one scene in which Horatius with his father, Celer, had confronted the rex, Tarquin. Kingsley wanted to get as much of that down on paper as possible. In actuality the event preceded the battle that had taken place near Tibur, but it was still quite clear in his mind.

He spoke into the vocotyper's receiver carefully.

It was the first time Horatius had met his rex and he was impressed. Tarquin Superbus used the Regia for his conferences and there the two found him, seated behind a table where he worked with various clerks and assistants. A lictor announced them and Tarquin looked up as though irritated by the interruption, but he answered the salute Celer Horatius gave him as commander in chief of the forces of the city. Tarquin said something to the clerks, who gathered up the materials they had been working on and left the room, leaving the two alone with the rex.

At this time of his life, Lucius Tarquin Superbus was an old man, though he was hale and carried himself straight. He was approximately seventy years of age, although he still rode before his armies in the field and was not beyond engaging in the thickest of the battle. But the years of pressure and responsibility had soured him and young Horatius found that he could not warm to the man despite the fact that, as rex, he was Horatius' ultimate commander.

Celer introduced the younger man simply. "My son, Phipe Horatius Cocles, who assumed the toga but yesterday."

Tarquin estimated the young man with his eyes, which were keen and penetrating and peered from beneath possibly the greatest eyebrows Horatius had ever seen. He said, "Phipe. It is an Etruscan rather than a Latin or Sabine name."

If Horatius had learned anything in his years in Caere it was the ability to remain at ease, secure in his own dignity no matter what the company or situation. He answered. "It was my great-uncle's name, sir. Phipe Camna, lucumo of Caere, who fell at the naval battle off Sardinia against the Phocaeans."

Tarquin's eyes narrowed thoughtfully, though he must already have been fully aware of the story and the Horatian background. He looked from Phipe to his silent father, and then back again. "Indeed," he said sourly, "I detect a note of pride, Phipe Horatius. Since my own family is of Etruscan origin, I am aware of their usage. Your relatives of Caere must consider you a member of the Camna gens and legally an Etruscan by birth."

This was obvious. There was nothing to say.

Tarquin's voice took on a curt note. He said, "Then how do you feel about Rome, Phipe Horatius? Or should I say Phipe Camna?"

From the side of his eyes Horatius could see his father stiffen and his mouth go white, which he knew was a sign of great anger; but Celer remained quiet.

Phipe Horatius had been highly influenced by what had transpired during the previous two days: his coming to Roman manhood, his being accepted into the Horatian gens as an adult, his assuming the toga and participating in the sacred ceremonies of his gens and curia. A young man can be highly impressed by such things. However, there was something else in the atmosphere of the room. Celer Horatius had presented his son and Tarquin Superbus had seen fit to question his citizenship.

Horatius said, "I am a Roman, sir."

Tarquin leaned back in his chair and his stare from beneath those shaggy brows was more like a glower. He said, "And suppose the needs of Rome were such that it was necessary to send our host against Caere?"

Celer Horatius' silence was such that it could be *felt*, and Phipe could only wonder how his father would have answered the question.

But Phipe had been able to say, "May the gods never make that necessary, sir. But I am a Roman."

Tarquin grunted approval of that. "Very well, Phipe Horatius. Your father has served Rome well, let us hope you will do likewise. I might mention that I have already heard of you through my son, Sextus. As a result of the recommendation of your father and my son, I am assigning you to the cohort of Marcus Valerius, despite the fact of your plebian background. The spearmen of the Valerius cohort are almost invariably drawn from patrician families and are in training to become future officers of the Roman host. It is deliberately sent into the most dangerous situations for the experience."

My father said stiffly, "We are honored, sir."

The old man grunted again. "That will be all, Phipe Horatius. Leave us. I have words to say with your elder, though why I continue to surround myself with critics of my policies I hardly know." His eyes were glowering once more. But Celer Horatius' face remained expressionless.

Kingsley Cusack had nearly finished his notes on this portion of the Horatius life when the phone screen rang. He activated it. The face there was that of the girl, Clara Maritano. She was as pretty as he had remembered her and as fey looking as before; her mouth was red, and again she wore a black turtleneck sweater.

She said pertly, "Good evening, Dr. Cusack. Have you considered our, uh, financial deal?"

He said, "Yes, I considered it."

She tilted her head slightly, in a very cute manner, he thought. She said, "Positive or negative?"

Something came to him. He said, "I'll tell you what. I'm a little nervous about this being on the phone. Why don't you come here and we'll discuss it?"

"Wonderful. I'll be right up."

It couldn't have been more than ten minutes before the identity screen buzzed. He was already in the living room, one highball in hand, another sitting on the cocktail table. He put his drink down and went over. He opened up.

She entered and said perkily, "Hi, King."

"Hello, Clara," he said. "How did you know I was called King?"

She spotted the drink he had ordered for her, went over to pick it up, and then lowered herself into an easy chair. She smiled at him mockingly.

He took up his own drink and seated himself on the couch, facing her. He said, "There was an electronic bug in the academician's escape sanctum, but I destroyed it and found out later that it had been placed there by another outfit than yours. So how did you find out that Bryce Norman calls me King? No one else does."

That had set her back for a moment. She took a sip of her drink. Finally, she said, "Why did you think there was only one bug in the escape sanctum, King? If you destroyed a bug in there, it wasn't ours. Ours is still operative. Whose was it?"

"I don't know," he told her. "Why did you let me know about your own?"

She shrugged her shapely shoulders, which made her breasts bounce a bit. She wore no brassiere. "It doesn't make any difference now. We got all the information we needed. What we need now is the dream machine. So what is your decision? One million pseudo-dollars for forty-eight hours with the dream machine."

He said, "The other group has offered two million."

She stared at him for a moment, then said, "All right. We'll meet that price and up it another one hundred thousand pseudo-dollars, for a total of two million, one hundred thousand pseudo-dollars."

She was seated in such a manner that her very short black skirt was hiked to the point of revealing the pinkness of her inner thighs.

"That's a lot of money," he said. "But I'm afraid that it's still not for sale." His voice was a bit tight.

It had been a long time since he had bedded a woman. He had the *memory* of seducing Carmenta the Vestal Virgin, but in reality the last girl he had slept with was a tourist in Merida, Yucatan. And it occurred to him now that it must have been a full three months before. He had been so busy in his last weeks on the Mayan job that he had simply no time for his sexual needs.

"Well," she said, a touch of mockery in her sensuous voice, but no reproach. "The hermit of Yucatan, eh? Wouldn't those Mayan girls put out?"

He didn't know what to say, and was slightly embarrassed. She didn't bother to pull the skirt down. Instead, she got to her feet and came over to sit next to him on the couch. Her face came to his and she pressed those full red lips to his. And her tongue darted. At the same time her right hand stroked and then grasped him, intimately. She murmured something into his mouth which he didn't get.

His member was already raging by the time she took her mouth away. Her voice was husky and her eyes sloe. She said, "Is that for me?"

He said, his own voice just as husky, "The bedroom is over there."

Whatever her motivation, and he knew that it was one of the oldest in the world—a woman giving herself to attain some materialistic end—her instincts were all at least normal. She obviously loved sex.

In the academician's bedroom, they stripped out of their clothing frantically. He found that the hair of her pubic area was as black and full as that on her head. She had a figure even more volumptuous than would have been indicated when she was dressed.

They sprawled onto the bed without taking the time to pull down even the spread. He mounted her in lust and drove deeply home, feeling his foreskin push back over his glans as he entered. She was amply ready for him, and wrapped her legs around his waist.

They climaxed together in a few short minutes, and then both fell back, in temporary exhaustion.

"My," she said. "Some professor you turned out to be."

"I'm not a professor," he said.

"You want to be though, don't you?"

"Yes."

"Even if you had two million, one hundred thousand pseudo-dollars?" she said, amusement there.

"Yes. Even if I had that much money. You see, I like my work, Clara."

They rested only shortly. Then, she said, the huskiness back in her voice, "Let's get this show back on the road."

They got the show back on the road and kept it there until toward morning.

They slept for a few hours and when Kingsley Cusack was awake it was to find her black hair on the pillow next to him, her dark eyes watching him contemplatingly.

She said, "Good morning, King."

He nodded, still physically drained in spite of the sleep. "Good morning, Clara. And thank you."

"Don't mention it," she said, grinning at him. "It was fun. We'll have to do a repeat, soonest. You're not as old as you look, and, for that matter, you don't look as old as you must be, if you've got a doctor's degree and have books that took you six or eight years apiece to write."

"You seem to know quite a bit about me," he said.

"Yes. We've had you thoroughly researched. Even beyond what's in your International Data Banks dossier."

"My dossier! You mean the complete?" He was indignant. "You're not allowed access to my dossier!"

"We have contacts," she told him cynically. "But now, darling King, how do you stand on acquiring two million, one hundred thousand pseudo-dollars?"

"The same as before, Clara."

"Why . . . you bastard."

"You didn't give any more than you took, Clara," he told her. "You were charming, and wonderful, but we had no deal going."

She stormed from the bed, didn't bother to go into bath before dashing into her clothes. He got up and into his shorts, to follow her into the living room.

She said nothing at all, though he could see she was inwardly raging while he let her out the door. You would have thought she had been raped. Well, that was that. What did she expect, capitulation simply because she had allowed him her body? Allowed him, hell. She had *taken* his. Weren't women supposed to be liberated in this era? What did they expect, for a man to lose all integrity, and everything else, just because they slept with him?

He shrugged it off and, still clad in nothing but shorts, went on into the dining room and dialed coffee. He drank two cups and then forced himself to dial a good breakfast. He felt impatient, wanting to get back to the dream programming machine. Time was running out on him. He wanted to experience more of Rome proper. If his assimilated memories of Horatius bore him out, things were coming to a head in Rome. Exactly when they would crack he didn't know. What authentic history he had studied on the subject didn't inform him on exact dates. But that trip on which Horatius had accompanied the two Tarquin sons up into Etruscan country was an indication that Tarquin Superbus was mending his bridges, and for good cause.

He forced himself to finish the meal and then went into the escape sanctum. He was anxious to pick up Horatius at a point not too long after he had left him. He wanted to experience the entombing of a Vestal Virgin and all that must have been entailed. It must have been a traumatic experience for the superstitious of that period.

Perhaps he should have thought of himself as a heel in regards to Clara Mantanio, and perhaps he did—a bit. But, hell, he was about to enter the brain of a *real* heel.

Chapter Fourteen

Rome—Phipe Horatius Cocles

For the sixth time, I felt the mind probe come at a crucial point in my life. And once again not only did it experience what I was experiencing but sought among my recent memories. Does this happen to others, and no one speaks of it? Is it the gods, at work—or play?

As Aruns Tarquin had suggested, it was not difficult to become captain of the guard. The rex, in relief, gave me the position immediately upon my return, and after I found that my father, Celer, had actually died under the dagger of a political assassin. But now that must wait. I had to deal with the silence of Carmenta. Happily, my taking the position of captain of her guard was not as pressing as I had supposed. Carmenta was being kept in the Atrium Vestae which lies directly east of the small, circular temple of Vesta and is not far from the Regia, in the Forum. The building is an impressive one: In a manner it is almost a temple itself, since the six Vestals are all but living goddesses and are so treated.

The six full Vestals guarded Carmenta and no one

else was allowed to come within speaking distance of her, not even myself and my men. We guarded her from a distance. Actually, my duty and that of the spearmen assigned to me—all against their will, due to the bad luck involved—was to prevent any rescue attempt, or escape, that was actually quite ridiculous, since no one would attempt such foolhardiness, and there was no place in all Italy where she could hide.

A week passed before she was buried.

Slaves were put to the task of hollowing out a deep chamber, and an artisan to the cutting of a stele which gave her name and the fact that she had betrayed Rome in the year 241 of our city. Vast numbers of citizens stood, faces empty, and watched the digging of the pit, and all were glum. Not for the death of the girl, but for the sake of Rome, since it was commonly held that great tragedy would be the fate of us all in the near future.

The ceremony of stripping her emblems of virginity from her took place in the Temple of Vesta itself with Tarquin Superbus presiding and the other Vestals standing about, their faces woebegone as though news had just been brought of the ending of the world. Indeed, so great was this blow that it all but had, so far as they could realize.

The emblems torn from her gown, still surrounded by her sister Vestals, Carmenta was walked to the pit which was to be her tomb and to the ladder that led down into the interior. All Rome stood there, lining up as far as the top of the Capitoline hill to one side, so that they could see over the heads of the multitude, and up the sides of the Palatine on the other. But there were no cries against her, nor thrown stones nor dung, as one might have expected against another prisoner on the way to execution. Rather, all were silent, and watched with sick eyes, for there is nothing more holy to a Roman than a Vestal.

At the ladder, Carmenta looked up only momentarily, and then, as though by accident, straight into my face. And though someone standing immediately beside me might have thought that there was nothing to be seen in her eyes at all, still there was something for me, a deep accusation, as though somehow, in some way, I should have made attempt to succor her—and had not. I kept my own eyes straight ahead, my face stern, said nothing, and betrayed nothing. Thank the gods that the girl had not exposed me.

As she climbed down the ladder, her robe pressed against her and it could be seen that she was pregnant indeed. Almost five months by now. The slaves, who had dug the pit, now covered the hole by which she had entered, after extracting the ladder, and began to pile great amounts of dirt above her, so that a mound arose. Thousands of Romans made themselves comfortable for their vigil, for until such time had passed that it was impossible for the girl to be still alive, full care would be taken that she not be rescued. Twenty-four hours a day, thousands of Romans would sit on or about the mound, being relieved periodically by family or friends, to go for food or other needs.

I did not stay to watch. Instead I was in a hurry to get on with it all. I hurried to the Vicus Juguaris, which passes before the Temple of Saturn and where I had left my horse, and I headed immediately for the Forum Boarium and the Sublicon bridge.

The market was empty, citizens and foreign traders as well being in the Forum to watch the ceremony of the burial of the faithless Vestal Virgin. I tied my horse and descended to the river bank, just south of the wooden bridge. It is here that the Cloaca Maxima empties itself into the Tiber and such is the stench and the volume of the slow moving water and sewage that there are no docks or other facilities in the immediate vicinity. Running inward from the mouth of the great sewer for thirty or forty feet is a landing stage built for the workers who originally constructed the mighty engineering project, and for those who might come later, for cleaning and repairs. I slipped and slid my way along this, into the darkness, until a voice called, "By the cast iron balls of Hercules, there he is! The great lover! The seducer of Vestals!" And then a huge amount of laughter.

I growled something in return, but there was a great relief in me, for I had not been sure that they would be here.

The hulking bulk of Astur and the lithe form of Mamilius came toward me, both grinning widely as though it was all a great joke.

"The boat," I blurted. "The equipment. You have them?"

They were in high humor, treating this wholly impossible situation as a great lark. And, aye! how I loved these greatest of friends who would drop all for comradeship and travel great distances to fulfill it, not to speak of losing their high offices or even their lives in such a desperate game.

Astur laughed happily and hugely. "All is ready. All is set. And you? Have you carried out your end? Do you have the plans of the sewers?"

"I have them all, from the archives. It meant but a bit of gold in bribes."

There was a lot set boat, wide of beam and meant for punting, at the far end of the landing stage. None of us bothered to comment upon the sewer stench. We made our way to the vessel. It was filled with pitch torches and now Manilius struck steel to flint and quickly produced a small flame. He looked at me, still grinning. The fool was enjoying every minute of this! Perhaps his new life with his bride, daughter of Tarquin, and the responsibility of governing Tusculus weighed heavily on him and the change was a relief.

But then I noticed too that both of them were armed with sword and dagger, and Astur, indeed, with that fantastic brand of the Celts, which an ordinary man could hardly lift. So then they obviously knew the task on which we were embarked was no jest but might well result in the deaths of all concerned . . . and probably under torture were we taken alive. Aye! Astur. Aye! Mamilius. Friends both.

A torch ablaze, we punted up the sewer for a hundred feet or more, and then Mamilius, who was up in the prow, called back to me, "You have the cursed plans of this Cretan labyrinth?" We pulled to the side and made fast to the stinking, moss-grown, slimy wall whilst I brought them from the wallet slung over my shoulder.

Astur and Mamilius held two torches over me high while I traced our way to our destination. It was not overly complicated, but the distance was long. "Let's get about it," Astur growled. "At this pace, against the current, it will take forever."

I said unhappily, "I am afraid that the Vestalis Manima or one of the other Vestals might well have given her a razor or poison or some other manner to bring things to a quick end.''

That possibility hadn't occurred to either of them and we increased our pace. We passed the major junction of the Cloaca Maxima, where the giant sewer which drains the Murcian valley between the Aventine and the Palatine, thus making possible the Circus Maximus, joins that which drains the former Velagrum marshes and the valley between the Palatine and the Capitoline hills, thus making possible the Roman Forum. We pressed to the left, and though the tunnel here grew somewhat smaller, the speed of the flow became the greater, and so slippery was the bottom, the walls and even the ceiling, that we were hard put to find leverage for our poles.

Nor were we alone in these dark ways, for in the early stages of our journey great clusters of bats could be seen on the tunnel's ceiling, and scorpions hung upside down as though waiting the opportunity to drop upon a victim. And everywhere were the bright sparkling red eyes of monstrous rats, big and greasy with the refuse food they found here.

''A dubious place for a vacation,'' Mamilius chuckled.

''Vacation?'' Astur snorted, finding some projection upon which to catch the end of his pole and pushing mightily. ''This is the hardest work I've done for years.''

Mamilius said, and there was an oddness in his voice, ''And where did you tell your wife you were going when Phipe's messenger came, calling upon you for assistance?''

Astur didn't understand. ''Velia? Why I told her that

Phipe was in difficulty. That he had made with child some Roman priestess who was supposed to remain a virgin during her office and that she was condemned and that Phipe needed assistance to attempt a rescue. But she had already known about Carmenta, though not that she was a temple virgin, and sent me packing before I hardly had time to get my gear together.''

Mamilius sighed. ''I can see that I should have married an Etruscan girl, rather than a Roman. Had I told Tarquina such a tale, she would have brought the roof down on both of us. Where in the name of the gods are we now, Phipe?''

''Hold it,'' I told them, bringing the torch closer to the sewer plans I held in my lap. ''It should be here. Somewhere here.''

We studied the chart with care, finally came to a conclusion, and anchoring the boat as best we could against the wall, fell to work on the huge tufa stone blocks with iron bars and chisels and with a gigantic iron hammer which Astur had brought. As we labored, I looked nervously up at the ceiling, wondering what would be required to bring the whole thing down on us. The work might have gone the quicker had we not been conscious of the fact that overmuch noise might well be correctly interpreted by those Romans standing vigil about the mound where Carmenta was confined. At any rate, we pried and dug and chipped and wedged, and finally, seemingly after long hours of work, had managed to penetrate to the earth behind the sewer walls, and now the going went the easier. We took turns tunneling, one working at digging, one passing back the dirt and dumping it into the sewer, one resting.

And after a time I became aware of the fact that we must have chosen the wrong start from which to work, since all was conjecture. We had penetrated such a distance that by now we should have found her prison-tomb had our calculations been correct. Blisters of cold sweat came to my forehead, for I had no idea how long the air in Carmenta's small compartment would last. And beyond that I was still upset with the possibility of one of her Vestal companions having given her the means to suicide to hasten the final end to which they had thought they were condemning her.

I had been working at the digging, but now I returned to the boat and the other two. I noted, with additional despair that our supply of torches was running low and that soon we would be working in the dark. I told them my fears and they nodded in agreement; evidently both had decided at about the same time that we had missed in our estimation of where she was located. I glared desperately at the engineer's chart of the great sewer. There simply was no other alternative that I could see. This *must* be correct. I stared in hopelessness at my companions.

Astur said gruffly, "We haven't the time to start a new break in the sewer walls. We must assume that this is substantially correct and either to left or right ten feet or so. Very well, we will start digging side tunnels branching to both right and left of this one."

There was no alternative. We started a side tunnel at a right angle to the one we had dug thus far, and began driving it as rapidly as possible. Time now was running out. Carmenta had been hours in her sealed prison and might well have already died of lack of air. And always there was the fear that she had devised some method of suiciding. What, for instance, would prevent her from shattering the vessel which contained her water and cutting her wrists with the jagged shards?

Mamilius said suddenly, "Listen!" He had been passing the dirt while Astur dug and the tunnel was so long now that I stood behind him and passed dirt too. Astur and I stood stock still, not knowing the reason for his command. Had the sounds of our work been heard above and an expedition sent up the sewer to seize us?

"What is it?" Astur growled, breathing heavily, since on his shoulders had descended a great part of the back-breaking work, neither Mamilius nor I being able to move the larger stones of which the sewer walls were constructed.

We had been digging to the left of the main tunnel we had first driven, but now Mamilius put his ear to the tunnel wall to the right. Suddenly alert to the possibility he was suggesting, Astur and I did the same. And, yes, some sound was coming through. Something was making a noise beyond our tunnel wall—how far beyond, we could not know.

I seized the shovel Astur had temporarily dropped and began ripping frantically away at this new spot and then Mamilius and Astur too, though we soon realized that we were getting in each other's way and they dropped back to shovel off the dirt I threw behind me. Within ten minutes, surely not more, my shovel suddenly plunged deep, finding no resistance, and then, in a great collapse, part of the wall before us fell away and we could peer into the chamber where Carmenta had been buried.

Her lamp had flickered out, the oil exhausted, so that now she sat on the edge of the cot that had been provided her, and her eyes, unused to light, stared blankly at our torch. What thoughts had gone through her head as she heard the noises of our digging, I cannot say. Did she fear the coming of some enraged god, or some evil devils of the underworld? Or did she dare dream of rescue?

So soon as the hole was big enough to crawl through, I pushed my way on hands and knees into her prison, gasping for breath after my labors. "Carmenta!" I blurted.

Even then she could not know what to think. The stench from the sewer which accompanied us. The foulness of our clothing and hair, our faces and hands. Only my voice must have finally penetrated to her as I lurched in her direction.

"Phipe," she said, and promptly fell back on the bed.

"Balls of Hercules," Astur grunted. "She's gone under."

Whilst Astur and Mamilius labored to make larger our entrance to the prison hole, I bent over my Carmenta and tried to revive her without success. This final climax to her fears and woes had been too much and she was in full faint. It was necessary that we lift, tug, and push her through the tunnel we had excavated, and to our boat. By the time she was there she was almost as filthy as we were.

And then we must sit and debate the advisability of attempting to repair the signs of our excavation. Mamilius was all for this, feeling that if ever the prison tomb was opened and found empty, the Romans would think that Carmenta had been snatched up by the gods and would make no effort to find her. Astur finished off the debate by saying that it would take hours to make such repairs, if it were possible at all. Besides, by the time such an opening of the tomb would take place, if ever, Carmenta and all the rest of us would be far away and safe.

So we allowed the boat to drift down the sewer toward the river, and at this point our last torch burnt out and we were in the most complete darkness. Not that this mattered greatly, since the current was toward the river and there was no manner in which we could lose our way. However, it was then that Carmenta revived to find herself held comfortably in my arms, though in pitch darkness. And she confessed later that when she had realized that she was in a boat and could hear the lapping of water, she had decided that she was crossing the river Styx. And since her last memory had been of me, coming ghostlike toward her, she had decided further that I must have fallen on my sword in suicide so that I might join her, and together we were descending to the realm of Pluto. And such was her quick terror that she cried out sharply, "Phipe! Phipe!"

"All right, all right," I soothed her.

And then the lightness of the opening of the sewer could be discerned before us and Astur and Mamilius began to take the measures necessary to halt the boat before it emerged full into the current of the Tiber for all to see.

Suddenly, Carmenta must have realized that she was not indeed, dead, nor was I, but that somehow, miraculously, she had been rescued. She knew neither Astur nor Mamilius, the first being a complete stranger and the second so grimy from his sewer work that he bore no resemblance to the personable young Tusculum chieftan who had married into the family of Tarquin, but she easily sensed that they were friends who had aided me and that though covered with filth they must be noble friends indeed to make such supreme sacrifice. She must have thought that the three of us had recklessly antagonized every diety in the pantheon and were thus doomed to a horrible mutual fate.

It was still an hour or so before full dark and it was impossible for us to move until there was no chance of being observed. Astur and Mamilius had been in the Cloaca Maximus since before daylight, and I had managed to enter it unseen because the forum Boarium was empty during the ceremony of the burial of Carmenta. But now the market would be filling again, and for us to emerge, our clothes impregnated with dirt, would have revealed to the first sharp-eyed observer our whole scheme. So wait we must.

I introduced Carmenta most fondly to Astur and Mamilius and she kissed them both, tears in her eyes. And then we held a council to reveal our further plans to Carmenta and to explain to her what had happened.

I had sent messages as speedily as possible to Austur and Mamilius who had come posthaste. Meanwhile, I had assumed my post as officer of the guard of Carmenta, with a double purpose in mind. First, I wished to get a message through to her that rescue was being attempted, though I soon found this to be impossible, so highly guarded was she by her sister Vestals. Second, it was of the utmost importance that she not come in contact with anyone to whom she might reveal by name. I could not know whether in despair, fear of the gods, or under some other type of pressure applied by the Pontus Maximus or the other Vestals, she might betray my identity and thus endanger our chances of rescuing her. I might have known my Carmenta better. A Roman, through and through, nothing human could have brought my name from her lips, even to the very end when she descended into her pit to face black death and I remained above, my facial expression unmoving.

Astur and Mamilius had brought digging equipment and the other supplies we needed, and they had secured the boat. I had found in the archives the plans of the sewer Cloaca Maximus and had stolen them.

But she was still in despair, thinking our chances of escape desperately thin. But I reassured her. ''Astur's ship anchors at the end of the Tiber at Ostia. We will float down the river tonight, with you disguised as a newly purchased slave of his. At daybreak, the galley will depart for Sicily, and the Greek port of Selinus. I have converted all of my father's estate into gold, and there we will find a new way of life. Roman shipping is in its infancy and there will be none come to that Greek city who know us, or, even if that coincidence happened, what could they do?''

Carmenta wailed, ''But Phipe, everywhere we go the followers of Vesta will hunt us down.''

Mamilius said gently, ''Fair Carmenta, the cult of Vesta is followed only by Rome and the cities of Latium. But not at all among the Greeks, nor anywhere else.''

She shook her head in disbelief. "But the goddess Vesta is everywhere. In every home. She is the goddess of the hearth, and surely every house in every land has a hearth."

Mamilius looked at me, over the top of her head and said most gently, "Carmenta, it is sometimes difficult for one who believes in his own gods to realize that there are others who do not, but have different gods of their own. The Greeks, in truth, have a goddess of the hearth whom they name Hestia. However, they do not have Vestal Virgins, nor would they be interested in one who broke her vows and fled to one of their cities. Particularly if the refugees were well supplied with gold."

I backed my friend. "We shall be free in Sicily of Vesta and all those who participate in the institutions of the Vestal Virgins. We shall be free, Carmenta!"

Mamilius cleared his throat. "There is just one thing, Horatius," he said ruefully. "You cannot go."

"What!"

He continued. "Not at this time. You will have to follow Carmenta later and meet her at Selinus. Astur and I have discussed this. You must remain and captain the guard about the mound where Carmenta was buried. If you disappear at this time, someone might wonder about it, particularly in view of the fact that you volunteered for the position. Besides, if customs officials or other port authorities stopped our boat or inspected the war galley and found you, what excuse would you present for having abandoned your post and taken off in such manner? Suppose, touched by suspicion, they examined the galley and its passengers more closely. Would there then be chance of Carmenta's disguise being penetrated? She is not exactly unknown, being a Vestal.''

Astur backed him. ''There is no other answer, Phipe. You must remain until all possible suspicion is allayed. You can then make your way by devious routes to Selinus where Carmenta will be staying safely in the home of the Etruscan ambassador, a kinsman of mine.''

I was still unhappy, but there was no sensible alternative. Astur and Mamilius had brought a change of clothing for Carmenta and various devices to disguise her, including a dye which would change her hair from honey-gold to black.

It was beginning to grow dark and Mamilius and Astur drew as far away as they could and turned their backs so that we might say our goodbyes. I held her to me, in anguish, dreading the idea of her making the voyage alone to far Sicily. I trusted Astur's kinsman; still the Etruscan ways and the Greek ways would be difficult indeed for my youthful Carmenta to understand. But there was nothing for it. Already, there were probably Romans wondering what had happened to Horatius, the guard captain over the immured Vestal.

We murmured the things that those in love say when they must part, and an hour went by in moments, and then Astur coughed apologetically and he and Mamilius approached. Mamilius said his own goodbyes to Carmenta, grinned at her, grinned at me, and then left the entrance to the Cloaca Maximus, though I knew he must be standing immediately outside.

Carmenta said, ''You are my love and my only love,

Phipe. And I will wait for you, be it forever, but now go, for you must go, and I am in the hands of your dear friends and hence quite safe."

So I turned my back and left her and as I passed Astur he patted me heavily on the arm and said gruffly, "Velia and I both wish it could be Luna, rather than Sicily, but Luna is too near, friend Phipe, and if some Roman recognized Carmenta, then it might well be that Rome would protest to Volterra, and international affairs being what they are, it is possible that Volterra might find it expedient to return her to Rome. The chance cannot be taken."

"I know," I said. I left the cave and joined Mamilius.

"We can't reenter the town looking like this," he whispered, "even though it is dark. We shall have to clean ourselves as best we can, and then hurry to your house by back ways and find new clothing."

So we squatted there by the side of the Tiber, Rome's holy river, and cleaned ourselves as well as possible.

Chapter Fifteen

Princeton—Kingsley Cusack

Kingsley Cusack came awake, shook his head, and emptied his lungs of air. It had been the most wringing experience he could ever remember having. Even more so than the battle near Tibur. He weakly disengaged himself from the box and slumped into a chair.

What a scheme. But he realized that he could never put it into a book. It would be regarded as fiction and possibly it was. He didn't know enough about the workings of the dream programmer to quite understand if the International Data Banks, combined with the Intuitive Computer, came up with the truth or just the nearest thing they could approximate to it.

Another thing he couldn't understand was the fact that not only could he experience what Horatius was doing currently but could assimilate his memories. Well, he supposed that if the dream machine could so realistically portray the actions taking place when Kingsley was supposedly in the Horatius mind that it could program the Roman's whole life as well.

He ate a meal, after a couple of quick drinks, then made his way back to the sanctum. But this time it wasn't for the purpose of getting down to his notes, though he had plenty to make.

He dialed security and happened to get the same sergeant he had spoken with the day before.

He said, "Sergeant, yesterday I requested that you keep a record and photographs of all persons who appeared before the identity screen of this apartment."

"Yes, Doctor Cusack, and we did so."

"Only one person appeared, a girl. Did you identify her?"

"Yes, sir," the other said. "She is a student, a junior. She lives in Apartment 932. She is registered under the name Clara Maritano." The sergeant hesitated and frowned slightly.

Kingsley said, "What's wrong?"

"Well, the name is a pseudonym, Doctor."

"It is! What's her right name?"

The other hesitated again, still frowning. He said finally, "Doctor Cusack, I'll switch you over to Captain Frisbe. He's completely acquainted with the case."

A different face faded onto the phone screen.

Kingsley asked his question and the captain said, "Clara Maritano, eh? Why do you want to know about her?"

Kingsley said unhappily, "I can't tell you, Captain, but it is a matter that involves Academician Bryce Norman and, ultimately, perhaps national security. He should be back in a day or two but meanwhile I'd like the information to protect his interests."

"Very well, Doctor. The academician is a personal friend of mine and I am indebted to him. Clara Maritano's real name is Clara Capo. She is here as a student under an assumed name because of her family's, ah, prominence."

"Capo?" Kingsley said blankly. "Prominence? I've never even heard of the name."

The captain twisted his mouth. "Capo, Capo. Her father, Salvador Capo, is don of the largest Mafia family in New York."

"Holy smokes," Kingsley said. "Why does the University City allow her to attend?"

The captain was impatient. He said, "Doctor Cusack, the Mafia families have come a long way since they made such a notorious name for themselves in the early and middle parts of the twentieth century. They no longer bootleg, since there is no bootlegging; they no longer peddle drugs, since narcotics are so strictly regulated nowadays; they are no longer in gambling since the government nationalized it. Above all, they are not involved in armed, or any other kind, of robbery. They've gone legitimate, Doctor Cusack, and into such fields as restaurants, resorts, nightclubs, and even into such fields as banking and securities. They've gone respectable, in short, and invariably they send their children to the best of schools. There is not a reason in the world why Miss Capo shouldn't attend Princeton University City. The school authorities couldn't keep her out if they wished, and they wouldn't wish. By the way, her father is an alumnus, and a generous contributor to Princeton."

"I see," Kingsley said. "Well, thank you very

much, Captain." He flicked off the phone and for a moment sat there staring at the empty screen.

He muttered, "Gone legitimate, eh? To a certain *extent.*"

But then it occurred to him that there was nothing illegal about what Clara Maratino proposed to do with the machine. Her people, for whom she was evidently the mouthpiece in this project, wished to rent the dream programmer by the hour to very wealthy men, most likely elderly, so they could enjoy programmed dreams. What was illegal about that? In fact, even her proposition to him, that he allow technicians to study the machine probably wasn't illegal. Possibly it was unethical, especially on his part, but he doubted very much if the device was even patented. Whoever had invented it wouldn't want the plans in the International Data Banks where they would be available.

There were some other angles, now that he thought about it. He spent the next few minutes locating Academician Bryce Norman and succeeded. His friend's face faded in on the phone screen.

The academician said immediately, "Confound it, King, this damned cruise ship has stopped at an island so small that it hasn't an airfield. We're going to start off again tomorrow but the way things look it will take me at least a couple of more days to get back. Very upsetting. Have there been any new developments?"

Kingsley nodded and said, "Yes, another group has contacted me. They offered two million pseudo-dollars for the chance to inspect the machine. Then the girl came back on the scene and met that and upped the ante one hundred thousand pseudo-dollars. Hell, I didn't know there was that much money. By the way, I was able to check her out. She's a member of a Mafia family, the Capos. Her father is the don. I think that means the head man.''

"I see," Bryce Norman said. "I assume you've notified security about all this."

"Yes, and they're giving me extra protection. However, I'm not sticking my neck out of this apartment until your return. I didn't tell them about the reason for the siege, of course . . . that is, the machine."

"All right, King," the other sighed. "Hold the fort until my return, though God knows what I'm going to be able to do about all this."

"One more thing," Kingsley said. "How many people are in on this project with you?"

Bryce Norman frowned at him but said finally, "Only six others, now. I told you of the two who used it and came to disaster."

"How many of them understand the workings of the machine?"

The frown was a puzzled scowl now. The academician said, "Five of them, the scientists and technicians that devised it."

"Where was it built?"

"Why, right there in Princeton University City."

"I see. And this one who doesn't understand the workings of it. Who is he?"

"Another member of the faculty, like myself. Neither of us, of course, are technicians."

"Is he interested in politics?" Kingsley said.

"Why yes, very prominently. How in the world did you know?"

Kingsley Cusack ignored the question and said, "One last thing, Bryce. Does he live here in this building? And, if so, what's his name."

Mystified, the academician told him. "But please," he said. "Don't see him. Remember, I don't wish my associates to know I gave you access to the machine. It was actually a breath of faith."

"I've already seen him," Kingsley said emptily. He flicked the phone off.

All right, he had a couple of more days. He was going to have to get about it. He had time for two or three more dreams. He'd take one for an eight-hour period, tomorrow, and then, in spite of Bryce's warning, he'd take twelve hours the next time. And that would be the climax of the whole thing. The siege of Rome by the forces of Lars Porsenna.

He looked at the vocotyper and began dictating. Thank God for the sake of his research he would be able to make extensive notes even after the academician took over the dream programmer again.

He worked later into the night than he should have, ate late, and then flopped into bed, exhausted.

In the morning, he crammed down breakfast, though he had no appetite whatsoever, and then made a beeline for the escape room and the dream machine. He programmed it for the eight decisive hours of the overthrow of Tarquin Superbus.

Chapter Sixteen

Rome—Phipe Horatius Cocles

And once again the alien mind invaded mine. And this time I seemed to detect an anxiety. It seemed, more than ever before, to search my recent memories . . . to be more interested in them than even in the past.

Indeed, my recent memories were full—and largely full of catastrophe. Only three days following Carmenta's departure with Astur, the news came through that the Greek city of Selinus, on Sicily, their destination and where she was to wait for me, was being besieged by the Carthaginians, by both land and sea. The Etruscans and Carthaginians were allies and undoubtedly when Astur's war galley was stopped they would treat him with respect. However, they probably would not let him continue to Selinus, even if he wished to, and, of course, he wouldn't. It would be too risky for Carmenta. But where had he taken her as an alternative? Certainly not to his home in Luna, since he had already told me he thought that city too near.

It was with great reluctance that I had accompanied

the Roman host, led by Tarquin and his sons, to invest the nearby town of Ardea. Above all the siege dragged out for weeks upon weeks, and how was I to know whether or not a letter from Astur, or even Carmenta, might not be awaiting me at my home on the Palatine?

The siege was a farce in my mind since the city was well defended by walls and had been amply provisioned by the Rutuli, or the Rutulians as some call them. Unless Tarquin was willing to sacrifice the forces necessary for an all-out storming of the walls, our case was a hard one. And since his purpose was to take over the city and add it to our domains, killing half the population was hardly called for.

The men grew bored and the officers as well. Indeed, the higher-ranking ones, such as the sons of the rex, periodically went back to Rome for a night on the town. In fact, Sextus Tarquin had done so the very day that Tarquin summoned me and gave me dispatches for the city. I gladly took on the messenger's role, since it would give me an opportunity to check my mail in Rome and perhaps receive information on my Carmenta.

After delivering the dispatches, I went to my home on the Palatine, but to my despair there was nothing in the way of message from either Astur or Carmenta. I slept late in the morning, since there is never sufficient sleep in the soldier's life when in the field and the comfort of my bed was beguiling after the simple quarters I had before Ardea. I slept late, and the alien mind was already there in mine when I was awakened by Quintilla, the aged maid, who entered my room fearfully.

"What is it?" I frowned up at her.

"The Forum. There is much noise in the Forum, Master Phipe. Something terrible has happened. There is a smell of hate and fear. I know that something terrible has happened.

A smell of hate and fear, indeed. However, it was time I got about my business, so I arose and took the usual light Roman breakfast, and jentaculum, in this case: some barley pancake, salt, honey, and some olives. I stood outside the door for a moment and although I could not see the Forum from this point, I could hear the commotion. Quintilla had, after all, been right; something drastic had taken place. I was attired only in my tunic and returned to the house for my toga. However, I didn't like the sound of the mob below and decided to attire myself in military costume, although this was frowned upon within the walls of the city, and especially in the Forum where Rome's business and political affairs took place. However, after all, we were at war, and I was on a military mission of the rex.

I made my way down the hill and started in the direction of the Comitium, where, seemingly, all Rome had gathered. There were nearly as many persons present as had been gathered in and about the Forum for the immuring of Carmenta. But on that occasion they had been quiet, observing such a dread evil in the history of our city. Now, all were talking, shouting, screaming, in such volume that nothing could be heard. I pressed through them roughly, making my way toward the orator's platform, my premonitions growing by the moment. I noticed, in my passage, that I was far from the only man in uniform, though there seemed to be no organization whatsoever.

On an impulse, I snapped to the first soldier I passed, "Fall in behind me, spearman, and call out to such comrades as you pass to join us. The mob is ever a danger and Rome must not be allowed to fall into its hands."

"Yes, sir," he saluted, since the uniform I wore, as a messenger of the rex, was that of an officer. Evidently a veteran, he didn't like the looks of matters any more than I did.

As we progressed, he picked up a man here, I there, until shortly there were some twenty of us, and now we formed into marching order and quickly attracted new recruits. By the time we reached the orator's platform, there must have been nearly a century of good Roman spearmen behind me, and the crowd gave way and some of the noise of their shouting fell off as well.

Lucius Junius Brutus stood there, a dagger in his hands, the blade red with blood. He had been hysterically addressing the mob before my arrival, whipping them into a frenzy; now he broke it off and glared down at us.

He shouted, "Armed men in the streets of Rome! Soldiers drawn up in the Comitium itself! Another example of the tyranny of the Tarquins. Would you put patriotic Romans to the sword, O tool of the hated Etruscans?"

What was the fool trying to do, set the city in flames? With the parties and factions the town now supported, one spark of violence would see the streets running blood.

Behind me the crowd murmured angrily, but thus far kept its distance, though a mere century of men was but a fraction of their numbers. I called up to Brutus, "We, too, are Romans, not assassins of our fellow citizens. We wish to know what transpires, and, if it is of such importance that all Rome must be here on the spot, why is the matter not brought up before the Senate?"

"The Senate!" he screamed, brandishing the knife and using it to indicate a large milling group which stood behind him, and behind the orator's platform. "Here is the Senate, with us, all those who have not fled to join the tyrant."

Marcus Horatius, my kinsman, and patrician member of our gens, sidled up to me hurriedly, breathing deeply as though his fat carcass had just run a mile or more. "Phipe," he whispered urgently, "Tarquin has been overthrown. The moment of decision is reached. Now you must take your stand, for all who are with Tarquin are against Rome, and all who stand for Rome call for the death of Tarquin."

I stared at him; gaped might be the better word. I could not conceive of things happening so quickly.

I said, "But what has happened? I was speaking to the rex but yesterday."

He whispered urgently, "That whoreson, Sextus Tarquin, abused the hospitality of the home of Collatinus and raped his wife, Lucretia, daughter of Spurius Lucretius, one of the most influential men in Rome. Lucretia, in her shame, committed suicide after pledging her husband, her father, Publius Valerius and Lucius Brutus to avenge her honor. The city is in turmoil. A third of the Senate had fled to Ardea to join Tarquin. But, on the other hand, rumor has it that the army has already broken up into factions and some are for and some against the vile tyrant."

Brutus was screaming down at me. "Let each man take his stand. Be with us or leave the city, Phipe Horatius, son of the patriot Celer."

Instead, I growled deep in my throat and mounted the platform myself. I shouted my message in all four directions. "Veterans of Rome, all you in uniform who have come with arms. Muster here before the platform, in ranks, by centuries. March!"

Brutus cried out shrilly, his eyes wild, "How do you stand, Phipe Horatius?" And the multitude that pressed around a thousand-deep in all directions milled about, chattering excitedly and some in trepidation, for the spearmen were beginning to respond to my command and were pressing toward where my century stood at arms and at attention.

"I stand for Rome!" I snapped back at him. "Now, get off this platform and go about your work, while we go about ours."

Evidently, he interpreted this to mean that I had aligned myself with his party and went off in great excitement to consult with the other senators and knights who were backing him.

I formed up my men and bit out quick orders for them to take command of key points in the city. I dispatched a century to each gate, and ordered that the gates be closed to both those who would flee the town and those who would attempt to enter it. A wail went up from the crowd at this, but I ignored them. The condition Rome was in at this moment, a thousand determined men could have seized the city.

When some order had been restored, and only approximately two hundred of my spearmen were left in the Comitium, I joined the senators and knights who were still more remindful of a group of women bathers who had emerged from the river to find their clothing stolen, than the government of Rome. Men of rank and property, their every instinct was not to take any definite steps which would actually change the status quo, for who among them knew, once you started swinging the pendulum, just how far it might go?

I came to the salute and barked, "The *praefect urbi* is present. Why has the Senate not convened to deal with the problem that confronts it? These people need some sort of decision, some proclamation, or in short order we're going to have bloody riots on our hands; and my men are a mere handful."

At this point, Marcus Valerius came riding up, his horse in a great lather. I knew Valerius to be a strong adherent of the Brutus party, but had seen him last before Ardea with the rest of the army. Evidently, he had gained news of the chaos in Rome and had raced all the way. My former commander flung himself from his horse, at the same moment taking in the manner in which I had disposed those troops available. In his eyes was the bleak quality which they ever held in action and which I knew so well.

He rasped at me, "You're with us, Horatius?"

"I am with Rome," I said, but within I didn't know myself what I meant by those words.

He shot a quick look at me, then turned to where his brother Publius Valerius, Brutus, Spurius Lucretius, and various others of the anti-Etruscan party were standing. They consulted quickly and evidently Valerius made the same suggestion I had, although approaching the idea from a different direction.

I could hear his harsh, brittle voice. "Make it legal, by Jupiter! Make it legal. Then we are the government and they are the conspirators. Convene the Senate!"

"How can we convene the Senate?" someone said in anguish. "Half of its number is not here."

"Good, you fool," Marcus Valerius rasped. "Those that fled would have voted against us anyway. We must control the number remaining. Convene the Senate, and we are in position to outlaw the Tarquins and all those who have sided with them. The city will be ours."

At least, as a soldier used to thinking in action and emergency, Marcus Valerius was unlike the flock of hysterical chickens he was urging on. And, since he knew what he wanted, and they were not quite sure, they allowed him to herd them toward the Senate House. And then, with a sagging feeling within my chest, I knew the important thing was over, and for a moment I felt qualmish, realizing the position that for an hour or two I had held. But I was a soldier, not a politician, I told myself. Let the politicians deal with their aspect of it.

Back in the mob, which was rumbling and milling again, I could hear someone shout, "The Tarquin home. Storm the Tarquin home! Loot the accursed Tarquins as they have looted Rome!"

I barked to one of the sergeants I had appointed to help officer my commandeered forces, "Arrest that man and bring him here. Use force if necessary."

Expertly, the sergeant with four men cut the man out of the crowd and hustled him before me. I said, "Take him to the Tullianum prison. He is charged with incitation to riot and looting."

The hostile murmurings of the crowd grew, but I no longer feared them whatsoever. I barked loudly, "Rome is still governed by law. There will be no looting. Why are not steps being made to convene the Curiata Centuriata so that the assembly of the people can act upon whatever measures the Senate decided to present?"

Marcus Valerius emerged from the Senate House and called me to him. He said, "Phipe Horatius, I have been appointed in the present emergency to take over temporary command of such forces as are at present in or about Rome."

I saluted him and gave him a briefing on how I had improvized a disciplined force and how it had been disposed.

He nodded. "Very well. You are in command of the Capena Gate. Repair there immediately. You have my orders to recruit whatever citizens you find necessary to defend your post. So soon as I can raise regular cohorts, I will send you one. Inform me immediately if there is sign of horse arriving from Ardea." He hesitated a moment, then growled, "Most of the Equestrian Order seems to remain faithful to Tarquin."

I saluted again and left for my post, realizing that I had been relegated to a comparatively minor position, since the new heads of state were not quite sure of where I stood. Not that I cared. They were the politicians; I was serving Rome as best I saw fit, in my own lights and what I felt were my father's.

During the following hours, events flowed so rapidly that hardly did one tradition-shattering development take place than another was flooding over and surpassing it. The office of rex was eliminated and, instead, two consuls were nominated by the Senate and approved by the Comitia Centuriata and finally confirmed in the office when they received the imperium from the Comitia Curiata, one of the few powers that body was still allowed to maintain. Tarquin and his family were banished from Rome in perpetuity. Lucius Brutus and Collatinus, the rape of whose wife had started the fire which had engulfed Rome, were elected the first consuls, the term to be but one year, and the duties largely those of the former rex.

Following that, it was declared that all official ties with the Etruscan Confederation were rescinded and in the future it would be considered a neighboring and friendly federation of powers but one with which we had no alliance.

I received a dispatch from Lucius Brutus ordering that individual Romans be allowed to enter the city but that no armed units of any size be admitted until it was proven that they did not support the Etruscan faction. No one was allowed to leave. Evidently, the new government considered that the city was strongly enough in their hands that they need not fear an internal enemy.

The order came just in time, for a multitude of the army which seemed to be breaking up into factions at Ardea, had streamed back to Rome and was demanding entrance. Tarquin's large body of horses were immediately behind them, and for all they knew he had issued orders to cut down deserters of his cause. They were admitted and we had news of the developments in the Tarquin camp.

Tarquin was said to be in a rage, but still soldier enough to realize that unless measures were taken, the Rutuli, under their rex Turnus, would sortie forth from Ardea and inflict a serious defeat on the Roman arms. Drawing together, then, those elements who were still in support of his cause, he broke camp and began an ordered march in the direction of Rome, his knights, largely of the Etruscan party, acting as rear guard.

When he reached the walls of Rome, Brutus and Collatinus and the whole remaining number of senators were there on the walls to greet him. As captain of the gate, I stood nearby.

His rage availed him nothing whatsoever; in fact, through his denouncement of them they remained strangely quiet, and I suspect they were gloating and taking pleasure in his helplessness; for now considerably less than half of the host with which he had marched on Ardea were still with him, and there was small chance that he could force the city.

Finally, when his fury had sent him into a coughing spell to the point where his aides took him off to rest, Aruns stepped forth and called up to us. "These are desperate times and the final results of your illegal usurpation are still to be seen. Meanwhile, however, we suggest a truce so that both parties may determine exactly what has transpired and what is still to be done.''

Brutus, who was as capable of a high rage as Tarquin Superbus, shouted back at him. ''What sort of truce, Aruns Tarquin? Your family has been banished from the city and can never return. Under no circumstances will you be allowed within the walls.''

Aruns controlled himself; he was not a particularly patient man either. He called, ''There must be many in Rome who feel our cause the just one. On the other hand, possibly among these men still under my father's banner are some who would consider themselves of your party and would rather join your forces. I suggest that for the rest of this day, the Capena Gate be left ajar and that anyone who wishes either to leave or enter Rome be free to do so.''

The new consuls and the senators present consulted, finally reaching agreement and Aruns' plan was adopted. It was a fatal mistake on his part, since in the first half hour it became obvious that although the Tarquins gained various adherents from the city, they lost many more. Those of their soldiers without strong conviction one way or the other—and these predominated—had families within the walls and wished to join them. They were deserting the Tarquin banner by the thousands. A few score of the Etruscan families, usually including women and children, left the city, including the family of Tarquin himself.

Tarquin was again furious and his small army took off to the north, and, obviously, to Etruria. Marcus Valerius stood beside me, and we watched them leave.

167

He said harshly, "Brutus is insane not to order out our forces to attack them. They will gain in strength from this point on, not lose. We should liquidate the whole Tarquin breed while now we have the chance."

I looked at him in shock. I said, "But it would be Roman killing Roman."

He snorted. "Do you think it will not come to that? Disillusion yourself, Phipe Horatius; this matter has only begun." He looked after the forces of the retreating Tarquins bleakly. "We are strong now, confound it, and should act in strength. A week from now it might be too late. It is obvious where they are going. To solicit aid from the Etruscan Confederation which, as you well know, consists of twelve cities, each of which is as large as Rome."

Chapter Seventeen

Princeton—Kingsley Cusack

Kingsley Cusack came awake, as usual after a programmed dream, emotionally exhausted. This had been one of the best, so far as his research was concerned. He had actually witnessed the overthrow of the Tarquins. Through the eyes and the mind of Phipe Horatius Cocles he had seen the end of the reign of reges in Rome and the establishment of the new Republic.

So much of his earlier dreams had been comparatively inconsequential. The playing at schoolboy games in Caere, the meeting and later seduction of Carmenta. Even the rescue of Carmenta, though fascinating, had given him little to be used in a serious work on history and anthropology. The battle near Tibur, yes, in spite of the fact that he wasn't particularly interested in matters military.

He went on into the living room and to the autobar and dialed himself a drink. He was going to have to eat and then get to his notes. He suspected that some of those memories sunken in the Horatius' mind would fade away, and he wanted to record them immediately. He started in the direction of the dining room, knowing he had to force himself to eat, appetite or not, and no matter how anxious he was to get to work.

But it was then that the phone screen on the living room desk buzzed.

He went over and sat before it and activated it. The face that faded in was that of Bryce Norman. He frowned and said, "For Christ sakes King, you look exhausted. Have there been some new developments?"

Kingsley sighed. He said, "No, not really. It's just that I just came out of the machine. And for the past eight hours I've been subjected to the most concentrated series of experiences I've ever gone through. I witnessed the overthrow of the Tarquins."

The other looked at him accusingly. He said, "You're overdoing. I warned you about that."

Kingsley said defensively, "I've got the machine now, I suspect I won't have much access to it after your return."

The academician said, "Any new developments with . . . ah, with the bad guys?"

Kingsley shook his head. "No. I'm holed up here like a hermit. Security is guarding me. They don't know why, but evidently a certain Captain Frisbe is a friend of yours, and I seem to have carte blanche with him as a result."

"Oh yes, Frisbe," the academician said absently. "Well, I'll be back shortly. We're pulling into Caracas tomorrow. I'll get a shuttle jet and will be seeing you in less than forty-eight hours. Bye—bye, King." His face faded.

Kingsley sank back into his chair. He could realize now what his friend had meant when he warned him of the danger of getting hooked on the dream programmer. In a way, he was hooked. Not on such inconsequentials as sex, or the thrill of war, or super-gourmet meals, or anything of that type, but on pure research. The last week had been the most fascinating in his life. He was a scholar born and this avenue had offered him an unbelievable opportunity.

And he knew that when Bryce returned he was going to get precious little if any of the use of the dream programmer. The academician was himself embarked on a research project that must be as fascinating to him as the Roman-Etruscan investigation was to Kingsley. It was a concession beyond the call of friendship for the academician to have taken off the two weeks earlier than scheduled to allow Kingsley complete access to the dream programmer, and he appreciated it.

He went on into the dining room and dialed himself a sandwich and a glass of German beer and forced himself to eat. Then he returned to the escape sanctum. What had it been, about a week since Bryce had left? To tell with his warnings about sleep and about eating and exercise. Kingsley Cusack didn't have the time to worry about such things.

He thought for a long time before programming his next dream. He was against wasting it on some such deal as the reuniting of Horatius and his Vestal Virgin. He wanted Roman history and Etruscan history, and their customs, their mores—the things that counted if you were going to turn out a book on the period.

He instructed the dream programmer to give him

eight hours of the life of Horatius, two months after the overthrow of Tarquin.

And once again, he didn't get what he had expected. He had expected to be in Rome still.

Chapter Eighteen

The Fanum of Voltuma—Horatius

The mind probe was with me again, and again it sought eagerly not only my current actions but my recent memories. Memories there were aplenty.

Several days before, I had been summoned from my post as Captain of the Gates to a council being held at the Regia which Lucius Brutus and Collatinus had taken over as their official headquarters in much the same manner as the rex had formerly utilized it. I entered and saluted and found matters much the same as when I had in the past been called before Tarquin, with the exception that there were now two men seated behind the table, and instead of the sons of Tarquin assisting and advising him, there were a handful of the more prominent senators and military chiefs present.

Marcus Horatius addressed me in his usual unctuous manner, as though being my kinsman, he was a close friend; but at the same time he treated me with a certain condescension. He said, "Phipe, a situation has arisen in which you may better serve Rome than as a simple captain of the host. We are well aware of the fact that you are of half-Etruscan background and of Etruscan education and hence not only speak the language but are related to well-placed families and number among close friends still other high-named officials."

I did not like these preliminaries. They seemed to be building to a new assignment to espionage. I said, "Sir, I am content with my position as a captain of spearmen. For this I was trained, and thus I can best serve Rome."

Collatinus said gently, "We consuls will decide how best you can serve Rome, Phipe Horatius."

I looked at him, but there was no reply to be made. He was my commander in chief.

My kinsman spoke again. "Phipe, undoubtedly you have heard that the annual Concilium Etruria is being held at the Fanum of Voltumna. Our agents in the Tarquin camp have reported that he is making his way there. The reasons are obvious; he is going to plead for assistance to regain his position." Marcus Horatius let his plump lips go in and out. "You have been in Volsini before, so that you know the way. You speak their holy language, know their customs, have contacts among them. Phipe, it will be your duty to attend this meeting and put before it the Roman stand."

I said, looking from Marcus Horatius to Lucius Brutus and back again, "The mission is a hopeless one. All sympathy will be with Tarquin. First, he wishes to keep Rome within the Etruscan orbit. Second, he advocates keeping the old institutions which still apply in Etruria. Third, he is an opponent of the Greeks, as they are. Fourth, he is a Tarquin, direct descendent of Tarchon, founder of Etruria and all but a god to the Etruscans. What could I possibly say to all this?''

Marcus Valerius, who was dressed these days as a R ·man general, leaned forward and took over the conversation; nor neither of the consuls looked at him askance. He said bleakly, ''Phipe Horatius, when your kinsman enumerated your attainments he failed to mention an important one. In the past, you have been utilized as an agent to Tuscan cities to investigate and report on matters military. You are experienced in this field. It is true that Tarquin will probably swing the lucumones to his cause; or, rather, some of them, for I have never heard of a case where all twelve of the confederation's cities acted in complete harmony. Your official task is to speak before that body, to present Rome's stand. Your more important task is to take note of who will actually support Tarquin to the extent of military aid, and to accumulate as much information as you can on the potential strength of such allies. I need go no further; you are intelligent enough an officer to realize what we need.''

I had been as happy as was reasonable, considering my anxiety over the fate of Carmenta, in my recent position as an officer of spearmen. For a moment, I considered refusal or at least begging off from the assignment, but then it came to me in a rush that the Fanum of Voltumna meet attracted the highest ranking officials of all Etruria. It was an affair that consisted not only of serious consultation between the lucumones but of great banquets, games, and sports, and a fete beyond any other in Italy. It was not to be missed if it was possible to attend. In short, *Astur most likely would be there.*

I came to the salute. "I shall be ready to leave in the morning."

The two consuls nodded, and Lucius Brutus, a trifle on the pompous side, said, "You serve Rome well, Phipe Horatius."

Marcus Valerius rasped, "Dismissed," and I wheeled and marched from the Regia.

The following morning I was attired as a fetial and consequently must ride in a chariot, followed by a small honor guard of four equites which was to conduct me to Volsini.

The chariot proved irritating enough so that at times when our party was away from the more populated centers, I changed from both my robes of honor and my chariot and rode a horse like the others, in spite of the fact that the more conservative of the knights of my guard thought that such action was on the irreligious side. As a fetial of Rome, I should have worn the awkward garments and rode astanding in my chariot all the way to Volsini.

Ride the chariot I did and prominently displayed my attire when we passed population centers, or other localities where we might be seen by Etruscan armed forces; for as a fetial my person was sanctified and they would not dare impede me, no matter how much their inclinations might be toward the Tarquin cause. We arrived at the sacred grove in which stands the Farum of Voltumna, after four hard days on the road and were immediately assigned tent quarters by the officers of the concilium. Evidently, we had been observed on the route and messengers must have sped on before us to announce our coming.

I dispatched my knights—all of whom had been chosen from those who could speak the Umbrian dialect which is the daily language of the vicinity—to wander about the giant encampment, to eat and drink at the booths, and in general to listen to the gossip. They had been well briefed on our primary task and I could only pray that none of them were traitors and secret adherents of Tarquin, for, in my garb as fetial, if it could be proven my real purpose was espionage, I would surely die a frightful death. As a fetial of Rome I did not leave my tent to mix with the crowds, for it was below my dignity. Instead, my guard brought me food and drink until the time came for the conference of the lucumones.

All at the conference were aware that the most important matter of discussion was the plea of Tarquin for aid, and so soon as the necessary sacrifices and other religious preliminaries were disposed of, the members of the Tarquin party and I were summoned to appear and state our cases. I drove up, as protocol called for, in my chariot, but with my bodyguard left back at my tent, for armed men were forbidden from being in the presence of the twelve lucumones in conference.

The twelve men lay about on their couches at their ease in a large circular building of wood which was artfully decorated and now festooned with local flowers. In the background from some source I could not locate was the inevitable music of pipes and lyre which the Etruscans seem to need for all activities. There were chairs, rather than couches, for both Tarquin and myself, which was a good sign, I thought. At least he was not being received as a fellow lucumo of the Etruscan Confederation. His three sons, Aruns, Lucius, and Sextus, stood behind him; however, none of them spoke during the debate.

My eyes went quickly about the room, even as I maintained my dignity as a fetial of Rome. Some of the twelve I could recognize. Aruns of Volsini, of course, my former schoolmate and Caile Camna of Caere, my maternal uncle. Pera Leprinia of Veii, once my host when I was on the tour with Aruns and Lucius Tarquin. And there was Porsenna of Chiusi, which we Romans call Clusium, level eyed, stern in his dignity, as befitted a soldier and statesman of his renown. I had never seen him before, but his reputation was such that I was certain that this must be he. And I noted with a sinking of heart Venno Satie, lucumo of Volterra and uncle of Astur. I knew him, since he had once come to Caere while his nephew and I were still students. My heart had sunk because Astur did not stand behind him as his marniu, but rather Avle Feluske of Populonia.

As a preliminary to the proceedings, the twelve were introduced to Tarquin and me, and we to them, diplomatic courtesy being extended to all for it was considered an insult to Voltumna, the god, to so much as raise one's voice near his Fanum, or Temple. All discord between men was supposedly suspended for the duration of the conference. Which was notable in itself, since the conference was for the purpose, largely, of ironing out such disagreements as had manifested themselves during the year.

Tarquin spoke first, and as had been expected at our meeting in the Regia, he made a good case for himself. From his view, a group of unprincipled usurpers had seized control of the city while he was in the field fighting the wars of Rome. They had taken power illegally, driven from the city the strongest of his adherents, and by browbeating, or by propagandistic lies swung to their support a portion of the remaining populus; and they were now in full command of the city and not to be ousted without help. He mentioned that under his party's control and with him as rex Rome had been an ally of Etruria but that the conspirators had broken all such ties, leaving the city free to form alliances with the Greeks or with whomever else they wished. I fancy Tarquin realized that the others were fully aware of this situation and did not have to be beaten over the head with the fact.

I spoke next, doing my best to impress them with the dignity of Rome's stand. How could it be, if but a minority of evil men had seized the city, that Tarquin was here requesting aid? Was it not well known that a government cannot remain in power against the wishes of the governed? A people deserve and want the type of government they have; if they did not, they would change it. Temporarily, a tyrant or group of tyrants may seize the government of a nation illegally, but he will not long remain in his position of power if the majority of the people are against him. If a tyrant, or dictator, remains in power it is because the majority of his people so wish it. If this is true, then Tarquin need not seek aid outside his own people, for if the new government of Rome did not reflect the desires of the majority, the two consuls and the balance of the new government would soon fall. As to Rome forming new alliances with the Greeks, or with anyone else, or in other wise posing a threat to the Etruscan Confederation, this was not so. Rome simply wished to remain aloof from bonds of alliance and to make her own way. It was well known that only some of the Etruscans had left the city with Tarquin, though all were free to do so. In fact, many of the most prominent citizens of our new government were Etruscans themselves.

I let my voice drop at this point. "I myself am related to some of you, but you see that I find myself in the ranks of the new republic, not those of Tarquin. This change of government is not an attack on Eturia but simply an internal affair, a change in some of our city's institutions."

But I could see how their minds were going. Tarquin, rex of Rome, had been overthrown and his office abolished. This was a most radical innovation and the lucumones must have been thinking that when such changes are in the wind perhaps they themselves would be discarded for the sake of new governmental methods. And there are few men in power who do not think of themselves as indispensable.

Fipe Arimnestus, lucumo of Cortina, called out to me, "But these changes in government are opposed to all the teachings of our founder, Tarchon."

I looked into his face. "Rome is not an Etruscan city, but rather a city of all men and composed principally of Latins and Sabines. The Etruscans among us are an honored minority, but a minority still. We must find our own way, even though Tarchon directed yours."

They shifted their positions on their couches, uncomfortably.

Porsenna of Clusium spoke to me courteously, "You are through, Phipe Horatius?"

"In Etruria," I said, in equal courtesy, "I am addressed as Phipe Camna, for I honor my mother's blood as greatly as I do my father's, and my mother's gens was the Camna of Caere. Yes, for the time I am through."

A trifle wryly, I thought, Porsenna said, "It is difficult to decide whether you present yourself as a Roman or an Etruscan, noble fetial."

He looked at his fellow lucumones, and said, "Some of the implications of what have been revealed to us this afternoon should be considered. It becomes ever more evident that the world is in change, and that it might well be that those who fail to change with it will fall behind—or beneath—in the march of progress. For progress there is in the world and even those who would cannot stay it. It might well serve us to consider how best we can adapt our own institutions to guarantee that our confederation will remain prominent, even foremost, among the world's growing powers."

"What might you suggest, Porsenna of Chiusi?" my uncle Caile Camna said softly and with an element of disagreement below the surface of his words.

Porsenna nodded to him. "Among other things, I suggest that our league be strengthened; that the ties that bind us be tightened manyfold, for now our cities go forth to fight our enemies one by one, and, if this continues, they will fall—one by one. What do I suggest? That we so unite as to be under one strong government, with one strong army and one strong navy to enforce our needs."

Fipe Arimnestus of Cortona, who was known to be friend and admirer of the able Porsenna, said aloud, "He is right, of course. As matters now stand, an ambitious power, such as Syracuse, could attack us and, in view of her strength, defeat us, if we meet her individually. Together we could defeat her were her strength fourfold."

Volnius of Arezzo said softly, "And who would lead this greater league of all Etruria, the city of Chiusi and its lucumo, Porsenna?"

Porsenna turned quickly to him. "No individual city need lead, and that man most capable and voted for by all would be the military lar to command our armed forces. How else?"

Someone said, soft as always in these debates among the lucumones in the grove of Voltumna, "We seem to have drifted from the subject of Rome and the assistance its rex has requested."

But Porsenna shook his head. "No. If our league was so strengthened, then Rome should be admitted to our ranks. And possibly all the cities of Latium with her."

I put in evenly, "That would be for Rome to decide, noble lucumones."

Porsenna looked at me thoughtfully, then turned to his fellows again and said, "It behooves us to realize that if we of the Etruscan Confederation do not unite Italy in the manner I have suggested, that it might well be some other will do it."

Aruns of Volsini laughed. He said, "Do you mean Rome? She is but one city."

"But potentially the largest single city in all Italy," Porsenna said gently.

And so the debate went, and from time to time Tarquin or I entered into it; but truly it seemed to be more a debate between the various powers of Etruria, rather than the two factions of Rome, and I began to wonder, finally, whether there would be action taken or not. At long last, a motion was made by one of the twelve that all in the conference room except the lucumones themselves withdraw so that the last words of debate could be said and a decision reached. So the Tarquins and I, and all those junior officers of the lucumones such as the marnius, the zilaths, and the purthnes, withdrew to the grove outside, some standing there for a moment, some making for refreshments.

Tarquin Superbus, erect and fierce in spite of his age and the pressures upon him, glared at me and said curtly, "You who pretended to serve me, you whom I honored by appointment to a patrician cohort. Traitor!"

I was an official fetial of my city. I said to him evenly, "I served the rex of Rome, not an individual. Now there is no rex of Rome. I serve Rome. I, and my father before me, owed nothing to you as an individual."

He glared at me, then turned on his heel and strode fiercely away; and, in a manner, I had to admire him, for he was ever inch a rex, though Rome's last. Aruns Tarquin looked at me painfully as though he would like to speak, since he, among the sons of Tarquin, knew me best; but then his shoulders slumped slightly and he followed his father, as did Lucius Tarquin.

But then to my surprise Sextus Tarquin came up to me, his dark face working in sullen anger. He said, "I thought you were a friend, Horatius. What in the name of the gods are you doing here, representing those traitors who have seized Rome? Why are you not with us?"

I said to him, "Better you might answer a question, Sextus, than ask them. Why did you rape Lucretia? It was the cut of her suicide knife that divided Rome in two."

His face darkened still more. "Rape Lucretia! It would have been as though raping a whore from the forum Boarium. She'd slept with half the equites in Rome—anybody who had a horse to ride out to Collatia. Typical Latin hypocrisy. They blather of their religion and their code of morality, but in private——"

I cut him short, but there must have been shocked surprise in my voice, for in truth I was already beginning to doubt that he lied. I said, "But she committed suicide, in view of her dishonor."

"Unbelievable," he said, his voice stubborn as of old when we were students in Caere. "The truth of the matter is I'd had too much wine when I rode out to her villa that night. When I banged on the door for admission, the whole household must have heard. Later, I spotted a servant, one of the clients, I believe, who had been spying on us. I couldn't catch the fellow and have no doubt that he took off and informed that lout Collatinus. Can't you see the result? Here the anti-Etruscan party, supposedly staunch, strait-laced Romans, have a scandal on their hands. The pure, virtuous Roman womanhood is suddenly revealed to be no better than the most free Etruscan women whom they've been decrying."

I could only stare at him.

He made it short. "Rape her? She practically raped me. It's my opinion the oversexed bitch was murdered either by her husband or by Brutus. More likely Brutus, since Collatinus wouldn't have had the courage." Sextus, his face still dark and disgusted, turned away and followed after his father and brothers, leaving me in my surprise.

I would have considered his revelation at more length, but it was then that I saw Avle Feluske of Populonia passing by. I hailed him, not knowing what stand he was taking on the Roman question, but anxious to speak. Fortunately, he had evidently either not taken a position as yet, or, in Etruscan manner, was philosphical about his country's enemies if he liked them personally. At any rate, he greeted me with obvious pleasure and mentioned the fact that his wife, Thupeltha, had been talking about me only the other day.

I said, "Avle, is Astur here?"

He frowned and shook his head. "He was needed to repel a Celtic raid."

I said sharply, "Then he's back in Luna?"

He said, surprised, "Why, yes, for some time." He still frowned, as though not understanding my intensity. "But he mentioned in passing that he had seen you in Rome. Now that I think of it, I never did understand what the purpose of that war galley trip of his was. Could it have been some official business in your city?"

"No," I said. "But, Avle, tell me, when he returned to Luna, did he bring a girl with him? A young woman, I should say. Perhaps eighteen years of age. Honey-colored hair . . . no, I mean black hair."

Avle laughed. "That he didn't. I am afraid that if he attempted to do so that vixen wife of his, Velia, would slice him into strips and the girl with him." He said, more seriously, "But you haven't received his dispatch?"

And the cold went through me. I said, "What dispatch?" My face must have been as blank as my voice.

He said, "Of course. I saw it myself. He sent it from Luna to my office in Populonia by a sailor-messenger asking that I see him on by the next departing ship for Rome. He said it was most urgent. Surely you should have received it by now. Undoubtedly it will be in Rome by the time you return. Though, the gods know, the number of pirates in the sea between Populonia and Rome are legion. I suspect Porsenna was right; we should have a united army and navy."

I said desperately, "You have no idea of the contents of the letter. Pirates, yes, I am sure. It never got through."

"My dear Horatius," he said stiffly. "I would hardly break open a sealed letter."

"No, of course not," I said emptily.

He looked at me inquiringly. And he said, "Do you really think that Rome can stand the combined power of all Etruria?"

I brought my mind back to the assignment upon which I had been sent, and said, "Do you think that it will come to that, Avle Feluske?"

He shrugged and said, "What alternative is there?

Porsenna was correct, we Etruscans must either stand together or we will fall separately. As you undoubtedly know, since the capture of Capua by that Greek bastard Aristodemus of Cumae, our towns in southern Italy and Compania have been overwhelmed one by one and the Greeks are pushing ever further north.''

"But Rome——''

He interrupted me, uncharacteristically impatient. "Rome has been our strongest bastion to the south. With Rome on the Tiber, no force could penetrate Etruria. But a Rome against us is as great a threat as a Rome for us is a defense. No, Horatius, we cannot allow the Etruscan party in Rome to be expelled.''

"What do you think will happen?'' I prodded him.

He said, "Porsenna is by far our best man and although there are various of our chiefs who are jealous of him, he will be elected lar of all our forces and be instructed to return Tarquin to his office.''

"And you think all twelve of the cities will rally to the Porsenna banner?''

Avle Feluske laughed in sour deprecation, and said, "Hardly. One city, say Fiesole up in the north, will contend that she is busy against the Celts and cannot spare troops. Another city, such as Caere, may decide that she has so long been a friend of Rome that she does not wish to join a military expedition against you. Still another, say Perugia, has long been a rival of Chiusi, and Perugia's lucumo has been a personal enemy of Porsenna, so in a huff will refuse to join.''

I made a mental note of this, but prodded him further. "From what you say, Porsenna will march alone against Rome.''

"No," he laughed ruefully again. "While some of

the league of twelve will be laggards, still the majority will rally to his call, since nothing else makes sense. And there will be large numbers of volunteers and adventurers even from those cities supposedly not participating.'' He added, almost apologetically now, ''I do not wish to antagonize you, Horatius, but there is considerable feeling in Eturia against the recent changes you Romans have made in government. You seemingly would destroy the very framework of our society.''

''Of Rome's society,'' I told him, the implication being that what Rome did in the way of changing her institutions was not the business of Eturia.

''But possibly of ours too, eventually,'' he declared glumly. ''Porsenna was not wrong when he said the world is going through alteration. Your revolutionary changes in Rome are all but identical with those recently made in Athens under Cleisthenes. They are not changes that we appreciate. Life as it is in Populonia and the other Etruscan cities is good; we would not see it otherwise.''

I said, ''Perhaps these changes are the march of progress of which Porsenna spoke.''

''Progress!'' he snorted. ''Horatius, I suspect you are so surrounded by Rome's multiple, interacting problems that you cannot see the single basic reality. No changes that undermine the freedom of men are progress.''

I began to explain to him that Rome's new institutions were a product of the pressures being exerted upon us, economic, social, and so forth; that they were not a departure from freedom but an attempt to maintain it. But then the aedilis of this Concilium Etruria approached to speak with me. Seeing that the matter was official, Avle Feluske bid me farewell and strode away.

The aedilis, a most serious appearing haruspex, saluted me stiffly and said, "Noble fetial of Rome, hear the message of the lucumones of the Etruscan Confederation in council gathered here at the holy Fanum of Voltumna."

My knights had drifted up behind me and now formed and stood at attention. "I hear, noble aedilis," I said formally.

He went on without inflection. "It has been decided that Tarquin Superbus, rex of Rome, has been illegally overthrown by a criminal conspiracy and, as an ally of the Confederation, is worthy of its support. Consequently, Porsenna of Chiusi has been elected lar of all Etruscan forces and has been ordered to march on Rome unless Tarquin Superbus is immediately returned to his office. Do you hear, noble fetial of Rome?"

"I hear," I said, my throat tight, "and shall report your message to Rome."

We saluted each other again, and he turned and left.

I faced my four equites. "Time is precious now. We ride immediately for the city."

We had all, actually, been expecting it, but even so the actuality was able to apall us. Rome, an infant among cities compared to any of the Etruscan centers, now stood not only divided within herself, but opposed to the whole Etruscan league to whom she had always looked as an ally, an older brother, an instructor.

Chapter Nineteen

Princeton—Kingsley Cusack

Kingsley Cusack sighed as he left the escape sanctum and went on into the living room for the drink or two he invariably took after a programmed dream. In a way, he was almost glad that he wasn't to have his full two weeks. He was working under such pressure that he wasn't sure he could stand it. He was working night and day, beyond the dreaming itself, and on top of that he had his worries about those who were attempting to get their hands on the machine.

He knew that Bryce Norman, with all the time in the world, didn't use the dream programmer the way Kingsley was using it. He would take on a dream and then spend as much as a few days taking notes and rounding things out before using the machine again. And he had time for his exercise and three leisurely meals a day.

Well, the academician would undoubtedly be back in a day or two and Kingsley could throw the whole thing in his lap. It was his problem. Kingsley Cusack was merely carrying the ball in his friend's absence.

He went on into the dining room and was about to sit down to dial his meal. But that wasn't to be. The identity screen buzzed. He knew damned well who it was even as he went into the living room.

And, yes, Joe's face, impatient, was on the screen. Behind him was Rocky.

Instead of going to the door, Kingsley hurried over to the desk and dialed security on the phone screen. There was a new face to him at the desk; a girl, this time.

Kingsley snapped, "Captain Frisbe please, and as quickly as possible!"

The captain's face faded in.

Kingsley said hurriedly, "The two men who invaded the academician's apartment and took me forcibly with them. They're out in the hall, before the door."

"Good," Frisbe said. "We've got two men staked out across the hall in an empty apartment. Stand by. I'll call them immediately." His face faded out.

Kingsley went over to the door. Joe was standing there, his face more impatient. He said something over his shoulder to Rocky and then pressed the buzzer again.

Kingsley just stood there, knowing the other man couldn't see him through the one way glass.

Suddenly, there was a commotion in the hall. Kingsley Cusack couldn't make it out, since the screen reproduced only at short range.

He flung the door open and then his eyes widened in surprise. On the floor of the hallway were two men in security uniform. They were obviously both knocked out cold. Rocky was standing over them; Joe was nearer to the door. He reached out and roughly grabbed Kingsley Cusack by an arm and pulled him forth.

"What's going on here?" he snarled. "The boss sent us to find if you were coming through, like you promised."

Kingsley collected himself. "I didn't promise anything," he said. "I'm not interested in the deal."

Rocky looked at the open door on the other side of the hall. Presumably the two inept security men had emerged from it.

Rocky brought two tubes from a jacket pocket and bent over the two fallen, injecting each one in turn. He then dragged them, one at a time, into the empty apartment. Joe continued to hang onto Kingsley's arm. The anthropologist struggled only slightly. He knew that he didn't have the strength to really resist the larger man.

Rocky came back after closing the apartment door behind him and said sardonically to Kingsley, "Afraid I'm going to have to give you another shot of dimout, Doc."

Kingsley shook his head and said, "It won't be necessary. I know that Academician Hans Braun's apartment is right here in this building. That last time you took me to him was a lot of hokum. You took me out of the building, drove me around a bit, and then brought me back. I should have suspected it sooner. Your being able to enter and leave the Longfellow Building without hindrance could only mean that you live here, probably listed as servants of Academician Braun."

"Now isn't that something?" Joe said, in mock

admiration. ''The Doc's got a real brain. You better report to the boss, Rocky.''

''Yeah.'' Rocky brought his transceiver from a side pocket, flicked open the lid, and dialed. He walked down the hall a bit and turned his back so that Kingsley couldn't make out what he said.

He came back and said to Joe, ''The boss says to bring golden boy here up to the apartment. We'll use the stairs. We don't want to run the chance of the elevator screens' picking up the fact that we left with the Doc here and went up to the floor the boss is on.''

They ascended the stairs, one on each of Kingsley's arms. He waited for an opportunity to make a break for it, but there was none. The apartment of Academician Braun was only two floors up from that of academician Bryce Norman. Which wasn't surprising; these levels of the Longfellow Building were devoted to the upper echelons of the faculty.

Joe stood before the identity screen and said, ''Joe.'' The door opened. They marched Kingsley through the entrada and the living room, to the large escape sanctum he had been in before. He glanced at the luxurious furnishings, the huge antique desk, the collection of medieval arms decorating the walls. The drapes weren't pulled this time and the room was nicely lit.

There were three occupants of the room, only one of whom Kingsley recognized. It was Clara Maritano. Seated beside her, in another straight chair, was a white-haired man of about sixty. He was impeccably dressed and had an air of considerable dignity and command. He was obviously related to the girl; they had facial resemblances. Both were Sicilians, of course, Kingsley thought.

The man behind the desk was obviously the same man who had been masked the last time Kingsley had been here. He had guessed at the other's features from the man's build, his pudgy white hands, and his voice. He had a fat face, a pouting, small mouth, and he seemed about the same age as Clara's relative.

Before any of the three spoke, Kingsley said, "Good afternoon, Clara. Good afternoon, Academician Braun. To what do I owe the honor of this second abduction?"

Clara said, "This is my father, Salvador . . . Maritano, Kingsley."

"This is your father, Salvador Capo, don of the Capo family of the Mafia," Kingsley corrected her.

The Capo don said, his voice smooth and cultured, "Our young friend seems quite astute. Which is always well when one is dealing in an important business matter." He looked at Braun. "He seems to have ferreted out both of our identities, though we were attempting to keep them withheld."

As before, Rocky had stationed himself at the door, idly leaning on it. Joe had taken a chair near the wall.

Academician Braun looked at Kingsley thoughtfully. He said finally, "Have a chair, Dr. Cusack."

"I'll stand," Kingsley told him. "I'm not going to stay very long."

"Very well," Braun said. "What is your decision, Dr. Cusack? Will you give us access to the dream machine?"

"No."

The Capo don said softly, "The two offers have now amalgamated. We have joined forces with the academician. You are now offered four million one hundred thousand pseudo-dollars to allow our technicians to examine the machine."

"It's still no go," Kingsley said grimly. "To someone like me, four million is no more temptation than two, or even one. Such amounts are beyond my dreams of avarice."

The academician looked at the Mafia head. "How quickly could you bring two strong men here?"

"I have four bodyguards down in the car pool. They have clean identity cards. If you okay them in the elevator, the two strongest could come up within minutes."

"Send for them," Braun said flatly. Then he looked at Rocky and said, "Those two security men you slugged and then gave the injections to. How long will they be out?"

"About six hours," Rocky said, "unless a doctor gets to them. A doc could get them out of it in an hour or so."

The academician said, "We won't need six hours. And we won't have it. Before too very long, security is going to wonder what happened to its two men and will send somebody to check. We've got to get into that apartment and pick up that machine bodily. Our four men should be able to do it. That dream box has to be transported up here."

"No, wait a minute," Kingsley said. "You can't do that. It's out-and-out robbery."

Clara laughed. "You've been in that dream machine too often, King. Your brain is turning to mush."

"That will be all, dear," her father said softly. He had brought his transceiver out and was now dialing, undoubtedly to his bodyguards in the basement.

The academician said, "Rocky, the doctor has a key to Academician Norman's apartment. Please secure it from him."

"No you don't," Kingsley snapped.

Rocky stood away from the wall and approached quickly. Joe just grinned and didn't bother to get up from his chair.

But it was then that the mild Kingsley Cusack, with his deceptively boyish face, exploded. He bounded across the room and pulled down a short cavalry saber, of the type once carried by the cavalry of Marshal Murat of the Napoleonic era. He spun with it and confronted the muscle man.

Rocky grinned and brought forth his switch blade and flicked it open. He went into a knife fighter's crouch and came in. It was a mistake.

The sword moved with blurring speed and Rocky's wrist was slashed to the bone. His eyes widened in pain, and he came forth with a squeal, even as the knife dropped to the floor.

Joe was on his feet, snarling. His hand went up and brought down an American Civil War saber, almost twice the length of Kingsley's saber. As Rocky melted back against a far wall, trying to stanch the flow of his blood, Joe came in, his eyes slitted.

But Kingsley smiled wanly at him and said, "What you don't know, Joe, is that I have the memories in my head of one of the best swordsmen that Rome ever produced. I recall all the details of my training in the crack cohort of Marcus Valerius. I can recall fighting with Etruscans and Latins, with Greeks and Celts and Gauls. This saber I'm carrying is approximately the same length as a Roman short sword of the days of Horatius. That one you have is, about the same as the swords the Gauls bore.''

"Take him, Joe," Rocky snarled.

"Yes," the academician barked. "Finish him off. We'd have to have it done later, anyway. He knows too much."

The Mafia head nodded mildly. "My men can dispose of the, ah, remains, later." He had paused in his dialing to watch the action.

Clara put her right fist to her mouth, and her face went pasty; but she said nothing.

Joe came in swinging. And Kingsley took no time about it. He parried the other's oversized saber and slipped his own blade through the other's right side. He could just as easily have killed the man. Joe fell back, his weapon dropping to the floor, as Rocky's had only moments before. He clutched his side and groaned.

Kingsley turned quickly and stepped over to Salvador Capo, who had, along with Clara and the academician, been rooted to his chair. The sudden upset in the situation had completely frozen them. Kingsley darted out the blade and flicked the other's transceiver from his hand and to the floor. He ground it under his heel, destroying the delicate mechanism.

Kingsley looked around for a moment, at the two wounded men and then at the other three.

"I'll be going," he said. "I suggest that no one try to follow me. When I get back to the apartment, I'm going to call security and report what's happened. Perhaps the group of you will want to, uh, if I remember my gangster terminology correctly, take it on the lam. You have assaulted, or ordered assaulted, two security men. You have also had me kidnapped. You have also assaulted me . . . with intent to kill. It parlays up into quite a charge."

He turned and left, bloody sword in hand. Rocky edged away from the vicinity of the door at his approach.

When he got back to Bryce Norman's apartment, he went into the bathroom and wiped the sword clean on a towel; then he returned to the living room and put the blade on the desk where it would be handy. He then phoned Captain Frisbe and gave him a quick rundown on what had happened. The captain grabbed his hat.

"I'll be right up," he said, "as soon as I can call a doctor for my men. What the hell happened to them?"

Kingsley said wryly, "The two men they were trying to apprehend were trained prizefighters." He added absently, "However, they knew nothing about sword play." He deactivated the phone.

He knew he would get precious little work done this evening, and while he waited for the security people he rehearsed the story he was going to give the captain. He decided to pretend that he didn't know what it was that the others wanted; that he believed it was something that Academician Norman had that involved national security, but he wasn't sure. They would have to wait for the academician, who would soon be home.

At long last, when they were gone, he went back to

his meal. He found it long since cold and threw it away and dialed again. Surprisingly, to him, he had no special aftereffects from his bit of combat. Perhaps his memories of Horatius had steeled him. He was glad he hadn't killed either Joe or Rocky.

He had to chuckle. According to the captain, Academician Braun, the Capo don, Clara, and the two wounded goons had evidently panicked and taken his suggestion. They had made a run for it. Damned fools. In this day and age. You couldn't live without your Universal Credit Card. You couldn't buy commodities and services without it. And every time you used it, the computers of the data banks had a record of where you were.

He was about to head for bed when the phone screen buzzed again. Muttering, he went to answer it. It was Bryce Norman.

The academician said, "Christ, King, you look all worn out. You aren't taking too much of the machine, are you?"

"Yes," Kingsley said. "It's a long story. I'll tell you about it when I see you."

"Well, that won't be long. I'll be back tomorrow."

"Tomorrow," Kingsley said in dismay. "But I'm just getting to the crux of things."

The academician's face faded.

Though he felt exhausted he went back into the escape sanctum and stared at the dream programmer. He had a premonition that his use of it was about at an end; that something was going to happen to prevent his further use of the equipment.

He sighed and climbed into the box and thought it out carefully before ordering his programmed dream.

Chapter Twenty

The Sublican Bridge—Horatius

I was standing at my post of duty as captain of the Porta Capena when the strangeness came into my head again, prying, peering into my recent memories, assimilating my every action.

The past few weeks had been eventful enough. Lar Porsenna must have been fully aware that the fickle Etruscans, who were the greatest of warriors when at the heights of enthusiasm, soon grew bored with inactivity or overmuch discipline. So he led them immediately to the fray. While his army, which had assembled at Sutrium, marched the thirty miles to the Tiber, her horse, led by the dark-visaged Verbenna, swept over the Campagna like a mighty rush of fire through dry barley fields. Verbenna's tactics were obvious to any soldier. He was striking so initially hard to frighten off any potential ally of Rome through sheer terror of the strength and ruthlessness of the Etruscan arms. Nor could our equites stand against him, particularly in view of the fact that a large portion of the

Equestrian Order had followed Tarquin and were now to be numbered among the foe.

A dozen towns fell in less than a week. At night, one could climb to the top of the Tarpeian rock on the Capitoline hill and see the line of blazing villages, red in the midnight sky.

I, with no more duty than captaining the guard of the city gates, grew ever more tense as the ill word came in. For hardly an hour passed without some horseman galloping up on his exhausted beast with still more news of disaster. Lausulus of Urgo, the famed renegade Greek corsair, whose fleet of pirate craft was known from Crete to the Balerics, had landed off Ostia and had taken Rome's port after a two-day siege. The Latin cities, as Marcus Valerius had foreseen, were either locking their gates against both Rome and Etruria or openly siding with Porsenna. The elderly rex of Tusculum, for years our strongest ally, had died; and Mamilius was elected to the office as all had long expected. Mamilius immediately declared for his father-in-law and led his forces to reinforce Tarquin and Porsenna, who hardly needed the extra troops.

But hardest of all for me was to stand, hour after hour, day after day, at the Capena gate and watch the long lines of refugees stream into the city. For a mile beyond each gate of Rome the throngs clogged up the way. In terror of the Etruscan bands of Verbenna, they pushed, crowded, and pressed, each attempting to get his own family into the safety of the walls. There were wealthy patricians in litters or chariots; poverty-stricken clients; free Roman farmers; babes in arms; mothers heavy with child; little ones lost from their parents and screaming their fears; flocks of goats, sheep, and cattle in charge of wide-eyed boys and confused yelping dogs; horse- or ox-drawn carts containing such family furniture as was portable; old men; old women; droves of mules and asses bearing everything from skins of wine to panniers of barley, from jars of oil to baskets of turnips. Cattle bellowed, babies cried without cease, goats and sheep bleated, mothers shrilled for children to heed them, farmers swore at recalcitrant livestock upset by the chaos, asses brayed their protests, chickens and other poultry tied together by the feet and slung over shoulders or by sixes into carts squawked or quacked their objections. And everywhere was dust, so that the first stop of the refugees was for water, as soon as they got within the gates.

A spearman standing next to me grumbled, "Happily, Servius Tullius must have forseen this day when he ordered the building of Rome's walls. So big an area did he encompass that we have room to support this multitude, animals and all."

"Nothing is happy in Rome these days," I answered him lowly. "With this number of people and beasts within the walls, epidemic will surely be with us."

The depression at this sight was so heavy upon me that for the first time in all my years I realized the truth of war. Not the brave warrior, horse plume at helm, charging bravely across the field to die on the enemy's sword in the protecting of his homeland; but the woman seven months pregnant plodding on foot through the dust, escaping the youthful cavalry band which had burnt down her home and murdered her farmer husband who would have defended it. Not the glory which is sung by the war note of the trumpet; but the terror in a babe's eyes as it toddles, shrieking, trying to find a parent who perhaps is no longer to be found. Not the cheers of the phalanx as the enemy banner is seen to waver and then go down before the victorious assault; but a half-blind old man stumbling along, bearing his bedroll on his back, his sole remaining possession.

And at long last, after my years of war and soldiering, I came to hate an enemy, for never before had I felt this. No, always before, had I been fighting barbarians from the mountains, roving bands of adventurer raiders, Celts to the north, Sabines to the south, or Latin neighbors, I had never experienced other than a neutral feeling about those men with whom I found myself at sword point. But now I felt cold anger, more strongly than any emotion that I had ever felt. Aye! Stronger than my love for Carmenta.

All efforts had been expended on strengthening Rome's fortifications both on the Janiculum, across the river, and of Rome proper. And finally even Marcus Valerius, patrolling the walls, expressed his satisfaction.

He stood next to me, noting the preparations that had been made to cope against fire arrows with water and dirt. And the large number of stones, greater than a man's head, which had been piled atop the walls to be thrown on an enemy below. The arrangements for boiling large caldrons of water to be poured down on scaling parties. The thousands upon thousands of arrows and javelins, handy to the footmen. The sacks and baskets of sand and gravel and rock which stood ready to be thrown into any breach or to strengthen any weak spot that might develop in the tufa-block walls.

Marcus Valerius nodded to me and laughed harshly. "We shall test the hearts of our Tuscan friends, Horatius."

"Not too soon for me," I said.

His eyebrows went up. "Do not tell me that our reserved Horatius has become at long last a fire-eater. I had always thought you somewhat wavering on the Tuscan issue."

My face must have darkened for he chuckled gruffly. He said, "Forgive me. With Rome in her present straits perhaps there is no place for jest." He turned to pass on, his officers following him, but then a horseman came riding up in excitement.

"Valerius!" he shouted. "The consuls require your presence at the river gate. The full host of Lar Porsenna is striking from the west!"

"The west!" Valerius rasped. "Don't be ridiculous." But he spun on one of his officers and clipped, "Get me a horse. The rest of you follow as quickly as you can. Commandeer animals."

"Sir," I said, "I have two mounts below."

He didn't bother to answer, simply followed me down a ladder to the street where I had the two steeds awaiting my needs. I used them to patrol from one gate to the other.

He didn't speak when I joined him in his gallop across the city, rather than giving the second horse to one of his senior officers. For my part, I did not know why I accompanied him, other than that the river gate, poorly fortified as it was, was my responsibility along with the other gates. In fact, I felt a sinking of heart, since on the river side of the city, Janiculum, on the opposite bank of the river, was our only defense.

By the time we arrived at the forum Boarium and the Sublicon bridge, the word had spread that Janiculum was under full attack and thousands of the people had collected anxiously to stare in that direction and possibly to seek what confidence they could in their elected leaders who were gathered at the Rome end of the great wooden bridge. Both Lucius Brutus and Collatinus were there, and they both looked wan. Already, numbers of wounded were falling back from the Janiculum heights and the trickle was becoming a stream. And already stragglers were beginning to appear amidst them, weaponless men who showed no signs of wounds but only shameful faces and shifting eyes.

Marcus Valerius and other senior officers consulted with the consuls and seemed unable to come to a conclusion. My own belief, and I suppose it was Valerius' as well, was that full support should have been dispatched to the beleaguered outpost, even though Rome's wall be stripped of all but boys and old men; for the issue was being decided on the Janiculum, and if Janiculum fell . . . what hope to save Rome?

And even as they debated, the stream of wounded and stragglers became a flood, and the bridge became packed with soldiers who had thrown away sword and shield the better to flee the battle.

I drew one aside, a spearman I had known from campaigns past. "Licinius," I demanded, "what goes on up there? Are the Etruscans over the wall?"

He had taken a bad wound in his right arm, over

which he now held a torn piece of cloth as temporary bandage, and I could not hold him long for he needed care. ''Over the wall?'' he returned bitterly. ''They were over the wall at first dawn. Some giant of a lunatic who wields a sword full six feet long managed to work his way up the outer wall during the night with about fifteen followers. How they avoided the guards, I cannot say. Most likely some traitor helped their passage. Whatever the reason, at dawn they were on the wall, signalling to their comrades below. We counterattacked immediately, of course, but to no end. I tell you that giant is a madman. Before we could sweep his small unit away, the others had run up scaling ladders and came pouring over like a flood of laughing, singing devils. The greater part of our forces had hardly got the sleep from their eyes before it was no longer a matter of defending the walls but hand-to-hand combat with Porsenna's picked men.''

''Astur,'' I said, so low that he couldn't make out what I said.

''What?''

''Nothing,'' I told him. ''Get that arm looked after.''

There was no ignoring the situation now. Our forces were in full retreat and so badly defeated that they seemed incapable of fighting a rearguard action. Throwing away their weapons, they ran at what speed they could command for the bridge and the protection of the Roman walls behind it. And it became obvious that the full forces of Porsenna were now on the Janiculum since cavalry came riding out to lance those wounded and fleeing who dropped behind.

The consuls had evidently come to a decision, and

men went scurrying in all directions. I approached Brutus and Collatinus to see if there were any orders for me.

Marcus Valerius, his face dark, rasped, "Put your men to work, Horatius, at pulling down the bridge. Axes, crowbars, hatchets, anything that can be used. If they overrun the bridge, they'll be in Rome before night."

I shouted orders to my sergeants, but even as I did so I knew the hopelessness of the situation. Our men were still streaming across, but already their numbers were falling off. And meanwhile, high on the Janiculum began to appear the flashing of well-shined helmets, swords, shields, and spear points. Lar Porsenna's forces were re-forming for the assault.

And was this, then, the end of the Roman republic? The Roman dream which had been held by Celer before me, and by how many of the Horatian Cocles family before him? Was this the fate of the great city which was to have brought unity in strength to all Italy, in the dreams of my father? A rage swept over me in thinking that Celer's life had been lived in vain. All the work he had done was being thrown away. But then, in thinking of Celer, I also had something brought to mind that I had heard when I had been about to depart into Etruria with the sons of Tarquin: " . . . *the bit of odd information you pick up at random could well mean at some future date the whole cohort of comrades with whom you are serving might be saved from decimation.*"

I muttered to myself, "Not just a cohort, but possibly all Rome."

I turned again to the two consuls and came to the

salute. "Sir consuls," I said, "the bridge is narrow and but a limited number at a time can either defend or attack it. Already our people are trying to bring it down, but from the look of the approaching Etruscans they will be here before the bridge can be destroyed."

Lucius Brutus glared at me testily, knowing the truth of what I said, but helpless to find answer.

I remained at the formal salute. I said, "Let me ask for two volunteers to join me and we'll attempt to keep the way until the bridge goes down behind us. It might hold them for an additional short stay."

"Don't be ridiculous," Marcus Valerius snorted.

But my kinsman, Marcus Horatius, said shrilly, "Let him go! Let him go! Even a few minutes can count."

For now our people were pouring in the hundreds down to the river side with axes and crowbars and every other tool to be found and with more enthusiasm than science were attacking the planks and props of the Sublicon bridge.

There were hundreds of Roman soldiers, arms in hand, gathered hesitantly at the Roman side of the bridge, most of them staring in dismay at the long lines of Etruscans who were beginning to descend the Janiculum hill. From far off we could hear the pealing of the trumpets, the clashing of weapons and shields.

I climbed atop a cart which had once borne produce to the forum Boarium market and shouted out, "Two volunteers are needed to stand at the far end of the bridge and attempt to hold the enemy for but a few extra minutes."

Every man within range of my voice drew his sword

and held it high, in sign of requesting the post. I looked over them with care, for I knew for whom I was searching, since all my plan depended upon them. I located them both.

I shouted, "Titus Herminius!"

He began pushing his way through the crowd to join me, and the crowd shouted its approval for Herminius had distinguished himself a score of times in Rome's campaigns.

"Spuruius Lartius!" I called out. And the crowd fell quiet as though in surprise and even Herminius as he came up beside me growled, "Why him? He's no soldier. Take Caius Mucius, over there. He's worth three of Lartius." Indeed, Mucius had been desperately waving his sword in my direction, volunteering for the hopeless task.

And, indeed, Spurius Lartius himself must have been taken aback by my decision, for though he had honorably volunteered for the action when volunteers were called for, he must hardly have expected to be chosen from all that number. Since the days when we had trained together in the cohort of Marcus Valerius, Lartius had kept himself in good physical trim in the gymnasium, but he had seen little action in the field, being groomed rather, by his family, to fill high office. However, he was by no means a coward. Armed now, as was every ablebodied man in Rome, he joined Herminius and me and even had the mettle to say, "Thank you, Phipe Horatius."

By now the Etruscans were near enough that individual banners could be seen and even individual chiefs and lucumones. There was Cilnius of Arretium on his celebrated fleet roan, and Tolumnius whose famous golden belt, which he wore in battle, gleamed in the sun. And there was dark Verbenna, leading his fast-riding horsemen like a demon of black death.

The Etruscan forces as always were drawn up first according to city and then subdivided into gens; for the Etruscan way was to fight standing next to brothers, cousins, uncles, and nephews so that emulation could be the word of the day. Each city had its individual banner, and my heart sickened to see that of even Caere, though her contingent was smallest of them all.

In the center and most prominent was the banner of Chiusi, or Clusium; and near it, carried in his ivory car, rode Lar Porsenna with ranking chiefs riding to left and right of him on horseback; and among them were Lucius and Sextus Tarquin. And when the Tarquin faces were seen among the Etruscans, a yell of rage went up from all Rome; for all Rome now stood on the river bank or lined the walls, those who were not working on the bridge. Even from this distance, one could see Lar Porsenna look up as though in surprise at the magnitude of the emnity so displayed. Sextus and Lucius rode on, unperturbed, and I grant that they were honest and courageous men by their own lights. ·

Herminius, Lartius, and I finished making whatever additional preparations seemed to be in order. We started across the bridge, three abreast, and I, for one, was feeling ridiculous in the face of the situation. Looking down, I could see the workers below prying, hewing, levering at the props and the planks; but their work was woefully slow in the view of the closeness of Lar Porsenna's host.

Chapter Twenty-one

The Sublicon Bridge—Horatius

When we reached the Janiculum side of the Tiber, we stationed ourselves to take what advantage there was in the narrow way.

Herminius turned to me and, a bit reluctantly, I thought, growled, "You're in command, if that is satisfactory with Lartius."

Spurius Lartius said nervously, "Of course."

"Then," I said, "I suggest that Lartius stand in the middle between us, for admittedly we are the larger men and possibly occasion will arise when one or the other of us can throw assistance his way; for cooperate we must if we are going to hold this bridge another ten minutes."

Herminius looked back and down, to check the activities of the workers who were attempting to bring the structure to collapse. "Ten minutes isn't going to be enough," he said. He hefted his sword. "Well, I never did like those laughing, smirking, Tuscan bastards."

And now they were coming in on us, the first rank

not pausing at the sight of us three. In fact, a laughing went up, for they were flushed with victory and were in a high state of enthusiasm.

A sergeant barked an order and some twenty men went into a spearhead attack, a formation in which there was one man with a hasta pike in front, two men with extended pikes behind him, three behind them, four behind them, and the rest bringing up the rear. They came running at us, full speed.

I could hear both Herminius and Lartius take deep breaths, for this was obviously very near the end.

But when I went into my plan. I took a full step forward, saluted with my sword and shouted, ''I am Phipe of Caere of the Camna gens and hence of lucumo lineage and challenge to personal combat a chief of equal rank!'' And then my heart paused in its beating, awaiting the results of my gamble.

The lead elements of the Etruscan army had already ground to a halt, awaiting the spearhead formation which was to clear us from its path; but now the spearhead, too, hesitated and stopped, the lead man looking surprised. Their sergeant, who bore the first pike in their formation, turned and looked to the rear questioningly. The spearmen behind, with growing clatter, began to bang on their shields with their swords and it soon became a great din, and I knew that the first obstacle had been faced. Long before, Marcus Valerius had pointed out that the Etruscans were warriors, not soldiers.

From the side of my mouth, I said to Herminius and Lartius, ''If I go down in this fight, you must each in turn issue a similar challenge, drawing out as long as possible each attack, for seconds now count.''

Herminius growled something in reply, his voice holding surprise, but the three of us could hear the sound of the wreckers behind us and all Rome lay in the balance.

However, the Etruscans knew what was about as well and two fetials came urgently forward from their ranks, talking hurriedly together as they came. One approached to within ten yards, knowing that as a fetial he was perfectly safe, and called, ''We know you, Phipe Camna, nephew and cousin of lucumones of Caere, but who are your companions that they should participate in honorable combat with chiefs of high rank?''

I called, ''They are Gaius Titus Herminius of the Titan gens which once supplied the Tites tribe of Sabines with their rex, and Caius Spurius Lartius of the Spurian gens which once supplied the Ramnes tribe with its rex, before Rome was ever founded.''

They conferred quickly, then the first turned back to me and called, ''But the Tites tribe and the Ramnes tribe have been incorporated into the Populus Romanus and no longer do they have a rex each of their own.''

''They are the equivalent of lucumo lineage,'' I insisted stubbornly. Each moment that passed was priceless, and I was willing to debate all day if they only would.

By now, Lar Porsenna, his ivory car swaying as the bearers hurried as best they could over the rutted road, came up with the first ranks, and he was obviously demanding to know what had halted the advance. He stared at the city, the bridge, the workers who were attempting to tear it down, and then at us three. By this time, the whole Etruscan army was banging its approval, and obviously such an ancient Etruscan custom could not be ignored by the lar of all Etruria. Porsenna bit his lip angrily, shot another glance at the workers beneath the bridge, then called out a stream of orders.

And forth three chiefs came spurring from the ranks, laughing and shouting as they came in great excitement; and as they rode toward us they shouted their lineage, one by one, to prove they were worthy of our challenge.

"Aunus, lucumo of Tiferum!"

"Seius, of the Leprinia gens of Ilva and nephew of the lucumo!"

"Picus of Newuinum, war chief of the Umbrians of Nar!"

Aye! Porsenna was no fool. Rather than allow each of us to fight separately, as I had planned, he was sending in his chiefs three at a time. Fifteen feet before us they flung themselves from their horses, drew swords, lifted high their shields and dashed in.

But we had two great advantages; we were fresh and they had been riding and fighting since early morning. Besides which, we were on the defense and were all veterans of the Valerius cohort and highly drilled in fighting in cooperation with each other, while they were probably strangers.

On another occasion, if the truth be hold, perhaps fiery Umbrian, Picus, would have taken me. But his reflexes were slowed with fatigue, though perhaps in the excitement of combat he wasn't aware of this. His first blow was taken on my shield and mine on his. He then attempted to swing a blow lower, to my thigh, but I countered, feinted in a manner that I knew the Etruscans particularly utilized and then, halfway through the maneuver, I changed the feint and came up quickly with the edge of my shield catching him beneath his helmet's chin strap so that his head was thrown back. I darted my sword point into his throat and up high into his brain, and whirled, even before he fell, to come to the aid of Lartius.

From the side of my eyes I could see Herminius chopping angrily at Seius who was down on both knees but refusing to take a death blow and fighting back. Seius! I remembered him well. He had been a fellow guest at the first banquet Avle Feluske had given for us in Populonia.

But Lartius was having trouble with the lucumo of Tiferum, who was a highly skilled swordsman. My companion had taken half a dozen minor wounds and was covering himself with shield and sword in desperation. Sensing my approach, however, Aunus spun about and his face showed quick despair as he took in the overall situation. Both of his companions were down, all three of his adversaries on their feet. He backed up quickly, his blade flashing against both Lartius and myself, and tried to avoid Herminius who was even now finishing off his foe from Ilva.

Herminius, ever cool in battle, grabbed up one of the javelins we had brought with us and threw it between the Etruscan's legs. He stumbled, tried to regain his footing as Lartius and I rushed him, then stumbled again and fell screaming into the yellow Tiber, which, swollen by months of rain, roared past beneath us.

Except for a minor cut, which I couldn't remember taking, I had no injury. Herminius had faired not quite so well and was in considerable pain from a thrust Seius had gotten into his left shoulder, so that it was difficult for him to hold his shield. In fact, after a moment, he threw it aside. But it was Lartius who had been wounded half a dozen times and was bleeding from each wound.

At the quick disposal of their champions, the Etruscans had gone from shouting and chanting battle cries, and frenzied excitement in general to a great hush. It had all happened in shocking short order in the eyes of they who were flushed with a morning of easy victory.

I stepped forward and called, albeit not so loud as five minutes before, ''I am Phipe Camna of the Camna gens of Caere and hence of lucumo lineage and challenge to personal combat a chief of equal rank.''

And Herminius called in his surly voice, ''Gaius Titius Herminius, of the Titan gens and of the lineage of reges and challenge to personal combat, a chief of equal rank.''

And Lartius yelled, his voice high, ''Caius Spurius Lartius, of the Spurian gens which supplied the rex of the Ramnes tribe and challenge to personal combat a chief of equal rank.''

Half a dozen of Porsenna's advisers crowded around his ivory car, that symbol of highest authority in Etruria. They were in high excitement, but I could hear his voice of command rise over their squabble.

And out of the Etruscan array three more came hurrying, and as they came they shouted their names and lineage. The first called, "Ocnus, lucumo of Falerii!" The second, "Lausulus of Urgo," and no more, as though all knew the name and rank of the boldest pirate of the Mediterranean. And the third called, "Aruns of Volsini, lucumo!"

Aye! Aruns. Schoolmate, boyhood friend.

But I had no time for reminiscence. The Greek renegade corsair, Lausulus, was upon me and he fought in fashion such as I had never seen before, and for a moment I despaired of victory. Using the tiny shield which he bore more as an auxiliary weapon than to protect himself, his long, thin blade darted in and out with blurring speed and it was all I could do to cover myself with short sword and shield. I had no time whatsoever to watch how my companions faired, though I knew that Aruns was against Herminius and feared for my companion in arms, though even at the same time wishing in anguish that Aruns could somehow survive.

The darting blade nipped me, here, there, though never so badly as to prove disastrous, and I fought on. And as Lausulus fought he kept up a running dialogue which was meant to throw me off guard, or perhaps to enrage or frighten me into a badly advised move; if we hadn't been in the heat of battle I might have been amused by some of his words, and possibly angered by others, but in combat we Romans are emotionless, and the words which might have affected the next man were all but unheard by me.

"Your wife is a whore, Roman, as all Roman wives, and I have heard much of her. She prefers oral perver-

sions, I hear, though sometimes she beds with a donkey
. . . Your younger sister is possibly a virgin, eh,
Roman? Tonight I shall toss her to my men. All of them
. . . Look out, there, Roman, you'll fall! . . . Your
temples, Roman. Tonight they will be deep in excre-
ment, Roman. I myself plan to piss on your household
penates. And as I do, Roman, I shall remember your
bloody corpse which I shall kick into the river so that it
will never receive decent religious burial . . . Look
alive, Roman! Behind you . . .!''

And perhaps it was this very running dialogue of his
that proved his undoing, for a man can devote his
attention to only so many things at once, and while
perhaps in the past such talk, while in the heat of
combat, might have given him advantage, it failed him
today. His foot slipped in the gore which had wet the
road from the first fight, and for a moment his eyes
widened in alarm as he tried to recover. I dealt him a
quick backhanded blow which severed his shield arm at
the shoulder, and a great gushing of blood spurted out.
He stumbled back, staring at the stub of his arm, unbe-
lievingly. He fell to his knees, and I stepped forward
quickly and cut his throat, though I should not have
taken the time.

I whirled and hurried back to the rescue of Lartius
and Herminius, both of whom were as hard pressed as I
had been. I took Ocnus in the rear, and in trying to
defend himself he was laid open to a panting Lartius,
who, breathing desperately, plunged his blade into the
other's kidney, for the Falerian wore only the lightest
armor on his back.

We turned to Herminius, to see both him and Aruns

sink to the ground together, their swords buried in each other's bodies. I bent hurriedly over Herminius even while Lartius finished off Aruns who was, at any rate, already unconscious.

I drew the sword from the side of Herminius and stanched the blood flow with a piece of his tunic which I tore away. His eyes opened, and he licked dry lips and shook his head. He pushed me away and stumbled to one knee, and searched around for his sword, though blood from a cut in his head was streaming down into his eyes so that he could scarce see.

My own vision was somehow affected, but otherwise I was the least sorely wounded of us three and fully on my feet, and I turned to the foe. I was too exhausted now to attempt to find out how far the destruction of the bridge had progressed.

I called out, my voice as strong as I could make it, but weak and shaking in timber, "I am Phipe of the Camna gens and challenge to personal combat a chief of . . . of equal lineage."

Herminius sucked in his breath behind me, and if anything his voice came stronger than mine, though he still knelt on one knee. "Titus Herminius! Of the lineage of reges . . . and challenge to personal combat . . ." And then his voice faded away and when I turned to look he shook his head at me apologetically and coughed and spit a huge clot of blood.

And Spurius Lartius, who never should have been in this position at all, not being of a warrior nature, called shrilly, "Lartius of the Ramnes . . . and challenge to personal combat . . . chief of equal rank."

And now there was full silence in all the host of the

Etruscans and on the river banks and on the walls of Rome. Though we could still hear the sounds of the wrecking, and if anything they had swollen in volume.

But the Etruscan host began to stir, and no longer did they beat their shields with their swords; for all could see that if the bridge fell they would not sack the town before the day was through, and that had been their hope. And an angry whisper went up and the advisors of Porsenna drew about his car again and their voices rose.

But then the ranks drew back and one man stood before the host, sword and shield in hand.

Herminius chuckled and fumbled on the ground before coming up with the sword which had been dropped by Aunus of Tifernum before he had fallen into the Tiber. He brought himself with an effort to both feet and called, "Welcome, Sextus! Welcome home!"

And even I felt sick humor well bitterly up from within me, and I called, "Don't turn back now. Here lies the road to Rome!"

His dark face was working in a rage, and he stared at the city walls and then down at those who were chopping the bridge from beneath us, then again at us three and the Etruscan chiefs wallowing in the blood and dust at our feet. And he stood there for a long moment, his dark face moving angrily, and then one of the Etruscan spearmen banged sword to shield and a comrade took it up. Sextus darted his eyes around, as though in sudden fear, and then shrank back into the ranks from which for a moment he had emerged.

Herminius laughed as heartily as he could manage and wiped blood from his eyes. Spurius Lartius was leaning against the bridge, his sword and shield both dangling as though he hadn't the strength to hold them up.

But now Porsenna bit out an order and the ranks parted and there stood the man I had been expecting, and long before this. On his heavy shoulder was borne the famous fourfold shield and in his hand the double-edged Celtic-type sword which other men could hardly lift. And a whispering went through the Etruscan ranks and again the banging of shields began.

But Astur looked about him contemptuously and bit out a command and the clatter ceased and all went quiet again. Then he stepped forward another twenty paces and called out to us, "Now listen, brave litter of the she-wolf. You have fought the good fight, but the issues are too great for but three men to stand in the way of victory. So now yield to the grace of Lar Porsenna and accept the honorable terms he offers you, rather than take advantage of your wounds."

I shook my head in negation, unable to find words, but Herminius was strong enough to call, "Come in and get us, Tuscan!"

Astur waited no longer, realizing full well that the bridge was rapidly reaching the point of collapse. He whirled up his sword, moved in with deceptive speed. Lartius, finding strength and courage from some unknown reservoir, stumbled forward to meet him, and Astur contemptuously, swept him aside with a side blow of his tremendous brand; and Lartius was thrown back a dozen feet before falling to the ground, as inert as a sack of barley.

Herminius dashed blood from his eyes and rushed in

furiously. Once again, I knew not from whence came his strength. For a short moment he traded blow for blow with the giant Volterrean, and I came in, inwardly sick at fighting with this, my best friend, but knowing naught else to do. But Astur was as quick in battle as he was strong, and he thrust hard and suddenly, and Herminius went down, blood welling in such quantities that surely it must be a mortal wound.

I had rushed in so fast that Astur and I collided and for a moment wrestled together, in close embrace. Behind him I could hear the Etruscans screaming their excitement at the new development, since two of us three were down and I must have appeared a pigmy in the grip of my gigantic friend-foe.

Astur growled at me, "So, Phipe, you prefer this to being with your woman. You prefer your city to the mother of your child who has sacrificed all for you!"

Even in this situation I could not help from gasping, "Carmenta! Where is she?"

His voice took on a shocked element, even as we wrestled, supposedly each trying to find an opening for a blade, and in this bout I had an advantage since so great was his own weapon that it could not be used in such close quarters. However, I knew that even had I the strength, I could never plunge sword in Astur of Volterra. "You do not know?" he muttered in deep surprise.

But even as he spoke, I saw Lartius lurching in, running low, a short spear in his hands. My eyes must suddenly have warned Astur, for he attempted to spin to meet the new attack and, as he turned, like Lausulus before him he slipped upon the surface of the bridge, covered as it was with fallen bodies, running blood, and even the entrails of those who had taken belly wounds. He slipped, fell sideways, even as he tried to recover and impaled himself upon my Roman short sword. At the same moment, Lartius, breathing in short, hysterical gasps, thrust him through with his javelin.

Astur's knees buckled, his eyes glazed, and he fell as a giant oak falls, so that the bridge shook beneath us, and my sword, embedded beneath his breastplate and running up into lungs or heart, was torn from my grasp. I bent over him quickly, tears running. I grasped his shoulder to shake him in vain effort to keep him from the journey on which he was already embarking, and I called something to him, but I know not what.

Even as his eyes emptied, he demanded of himself one last gigantic effort and winning, muttered, "Carthage"; then he looked fully into the face of black death.

I came to my feet, without looking down, and said to Spurius Lartius, my voice strangely even, "Get Herminius back, or he will bleed to death in moments. Here, I'll help you."

We hoisted Herminius, who was only partially conscious, to his feet and I gave them an initial push, so that Herminius started back across the creaking, shaking bridge, the arms of Lartius about the larger man.

And now that happened which I could never admit could happen. For I drew upon reserves I had not, as though the gods had suddenly granted me new powers. And I was as strong as I had been twenty minutes before, and I was as though my wounds meant nothing. And I looked around me for a weapon and saw my sword still embedded in my dearest friend and knew that I could never touch it again. Instead, I stooped and picked up the giant brand of Astur.

I had handled it before, but always it had been all my strength could manage merely to pick it up with both hands; nor had I the ability to wield it at all. It had been a standing joke between Astur and me. But now I held it in my right hand, and I swung it, point forward somewhat, to clear the ground, back and forth as though a pendulum.

And I looked to the Etruscan host and called, cheerfully, "What bold lucumo comes next, to taste our Roman wine?"

And their ranks were silent, for there at my feet were the noblest and bravest of all Etruria. Not that there lacked brave men and strong among them, for all Etruria's finest were here. But there comes a point in the bravest man's heart where the realization of inevitable death strikes him deep and within he cowers at the eventuality. And so it was now; and there seemed a chill upon the air, as though the spirit of death was everywhere around us and thirsting for the warm blood of men.

And I called out again, making my voice ring with contempt, "I am Phipe Horatius, of plebian family, but a Roman, and challenge to combat any with pretentions of equal rank."

And the lines of the Etruscans emitted a long sighing, but there was no movement, no laughter, no singing or chanting of battle cries, no banging upon shields.

Then Lar Porsenna, his face furious in anger, stepped down from his ivory car and, scarcely looking, pulled from its sheath the sword of one of his body-guards. Shaking off the detaining hands of his officers and advisers, he called to me, "Porsenna of Chiusi, and of equal rank to you, Roman!" And he stepped out before his host of the picked troops of all Eturia and walked toward me, a man now in his middle fifties, but even of step and eye, and proud in his dignity.

It was then that the bridge collapsed behind me with a deafening roar.

All eyes left our human drama and went to the wreckage which for a moment held there in the yellow water; but then, so fast ran the stream the dam broke, and plank, pier, and post went rushing for the sea. I stood there at the river's edge and stared down, emotionlessly; for we had won. Then I turned back and looked at the foe.

Porsenna called, in dignity, "Now yield, Phipe Horatius. Yield to our grace."

But there was mixed feeling now amongst those men who had been thwarted in taking the city after such early success against Janiculum, and a javelin flung past me, missing by mere inches, and a stone from a sling banged against my shield, forcing me back a step. I shook my head at Porsenna, though I knew I would receive the utmost of honorable surrender from him, and I turned back to the river.

I dropped the suddenly overly heavy sword of Astur, dropped my shield, and flung my battered helmet from my head. Without another thought, for had I thought I might not have acted, I threw myself into the flooded stream.

There is little more that I remember. The Tiber,

never a gentle river, was swollen with months of rain and as fast flowing as I have ever seen it. And I was heavy with armor, weak from wounds and spent with my exertions. Vaguely I remember my head coming to the surface, as my body rolled in the yellow stream, and my eyes faced the left bank and I could see the Etruscans in their thousands lining it; and when my head appeared, instead of casting javelins or shooting arrows at me, *they cheered!* But then blackness rolled in on me, even as I felt the alien mind leave me, though at the same moment I vaguely recall hands grasping me and being pulled, pushed, dragged and carried. I knew or cared not where.

Aftermath

Bryce Norman heard him through in detail, generally looking sad. When it was all told, the academician came to his feet and went over to the autobar and refreshed their drinks. He returned and sat there for a while, thinking it all over.

Finally, he said, "King, would you like one last programmed dream, to check out what happened to Horatius?"

Kingsley Cusack shook his head. "No, not really. It's not necessary. I suspect I know what happened to him. He made his way to Carthage, somehow or other, and there found his woman and their child. They could never return to Rome . . . not in view of the fact that she was a condemned Vestal Virgin. Besides that, he was becoming disillusioned with his city. The expulsion of the Tarquins, though he felt it necessary, didn't mean that the patrician class which took over were any more altruistic. The rich were already becoming richer, the plebians poorer. No, he and Carmenta would have to find another abode and he was a high-survival type. I am sure that they did."

"Very well," the academician said. "And I can cut my researches into Cyrus at the point where he captured Babylon. It was the climax of his life."

He came to his feet and took up a heavy paperweight from his desk and went over to the dream programmer. He began smashing the delicate parts.

"Holy smokes!" Kingsley blurted. "You can't do that!"

The academician came back and tossed the paperweight to the desk. "Yes, I can," he said. "It had to be done. The world is not ready for the thing."

Kingsley stared at him, still in horror.

Bryce Norman said wearily, "How long would it be before the Capo people—or someone else—made another attempt on it? Or, I don't know what's happened to Braun. The sonofabitch has gone to ground, somewhere or other. But it's no mistake that he was the dean of law studies here. He's a hard and very intelligent man. There is no reason that he wouldn't spread the knowledge of the existence of the dream programmer if it suited his ends."

Kingsley scowled. "How about your other five associates, the ones who originally built it, the scientists and technicians? They could build another one, tomorrow, I assume."

But Bryce Norman shook his head negatively. He said, "No. They are men of highest integrity. When I tell them the story, they'll support me. This device the world is not as yet ready for."

"As yet! When will it ever be?"

Academician Bryce Norman stared off, unseeingly, into a far future. "When the world has gotten to a point

228

where money is no longer a factor. When it is impossible for one man, or group, to control what two hundred million pseduo-dollars now represents. When men no longer exist who are willing to spend, perhaps, a hundred thousand pseudo-dollars so that they can dream exotic dreams. When there are no longer political groups that would practice secret spying and, what would amount to blackmail, to gain their selfish political ends. Until then, this invention must be suppressed."

Kingsley said cynically, "You can no more uninvent an invention that has once been invented than you can unscramble scrambled eggs. Somebody else will come up with it in short order. Given the International Data Banks and the Intuitive Computer, it's a sure thing."

"Then God help us," the academician said.

FRITZ LEIBER

6H

ISAAC ASIMOV